by MARY McCALLUM
Illustrations by ANNIE HAYWARD

GECKO PRESS

For my dappled children.—M.M.

For my family…everywhere.—A.H.

First American edition published in 2014 by Gecko Press USA,
an imprint of Gecko Press Ltd

Distributed in the United States and Canada by
Lerner Publishing Group, Inc.
241 First Avenue North
Minneapolis, MN 55401 USA
www.lernerbooks.com

A catalog record for this book is available from the
US Library of Congress

This edition first published in 2014 by Gecko Press
PO Box 9335, Marion Square, Wellington 6141, New Zealand
info@geckopress.com

Gecko Press acknowledges the generous support of
Creative New Zealand

creative nz
ARTS COUNCIL OF NEW ZEALAND TOI AOTEAROA

Design by Vida & Luke Kelly, New Zealand
Printed in China by Everbest Printing Co Ltd,
an accredited ISO 14001 & FSC certified printer

ISBN hardback: 978-1-877579-95-0
ISBN paperback: 978-1-877579-91-2
ISBN e-book (MOBI): 978-1-927271-16-2
ISBN e-book (EPUB): 978-1-927271-15-5

For more curiously good books, visit www.geckopress.com

Contents

List of colour illustrations

CHAPTER 1

A leaf

A leaf is just the beginning. Look closely and you will see it is leading you to a branch, and from that branch to another branch, and from a branch to a face. Annie had seen the faces in the hedge at the end of her garden since her father had brought the family to live in Winding Cottage. It was winter then, so she hadn't gone for a closer look, but when it got warmer she found herself walking past the hedge one day and, without meaning to, she was inside it. That's why she knew about the faces.

Now it was summer and hot. The sun made her feet heavy and her head droop like a sunflower. Annie knew if she didn't move quickly she'd be made to lie down inside and read a book, which was like being four again. Robbie, who was four, was asleep on the couch, his mouth wide open, a half-eaten honey sandwich squeezing through his fingers. It was the earthquake that had made them tired, shaking them awake just as the sun was coming up and the first birds were starting to sing.

It was a rattler, not a roller—not big enough to break anything, but big enough to get them all out of bed and standing under door frames in case the roof fell in. Annie had been woken by the knives and forks chattering in the drawers in the kitchen and Robbie's Matchbox cars making noises as if they were about to drive out of his bedroom and along the hallway. But it all stopped quickly enough and the birds started up again, and Annie and Robbie went yawning back to bed. Or rather they went back to their mother's bed. With their father working up at the lighthouse, there was plenty of room there.

Annie wasn't tired now, she was hot. What she needed was to be somewhere cool.

"I'm going to play in the hedge," she said, leaning

around the kitchen door, both feet on the porch outside, ready to go.

Annie's mother was sitting at the kitchen table, knitting socks for Annie's dad to wear at the lighthouse in winter. They needed to be warm and they needed to be red. Red wool kept your feet warmer, said Annie's mother. So a ball of raspberry wool sat in her lap like a raspberry cat and on the table in front of her was a large pink teacup. Beside the teacup was a teapot with a knitted cover and a crossword-puzzle book.

"Here's one for you, Annie," she said without looking up, "12 across: celestial body starting with *s*—four letters."

"Star."

Annie's mother smacked her lips like a kiss. "Star," she said, and wrote the letters into the boxes one by one. "Okay, 4 down. Eight letters and *e* is the second letter—"

Annie started to move but her mother held up her hand: "Stop." She wasn't looking at Annie, she was looking at the kitchen clock. "Your dad should be back from the lighthouse by now."

"Oh," said Annie. She was torn now between waiting and not waiting. She looked at her toes: *go, not go, go, not go*...one of them wiggled, all on its own.

"He's late. I wonder if the earthquake caused problems." Annie's mother put down her pencil and looked at the clock again, then picked up the knitting. Annie watched her fingers: under-over-through-and-off.

"It was a rattler, Ma. Nothing big. He's just busy."

Go, not go, go, not go...wiggle. Could toes move without being told to? *Under-over-through-and*...wiggle. They were telling her something.

"A lighthouse shakes more than the house, especially up at the very top," said Annie's mother. She was looking towards the window as if she'd heard Annie's dad wheeling his bicycle in through the gate. Annie listened, too. There was definitely something—the sort of thud-kerplump of his boots on the path—but it stopped as soon as it started.

Her mother was looking straight at Annie now. Her eyes were so green it looked like she'd been swimming. Some days they didn't look green at all. "You must be missing him," she said. Which made something inside Annie go thud-kerplump.

"I am." She hadn't thought about it, but now Annie realized it was true. Since Lew, the assistant lighthouse keeper, had broken his leg, her dad had to spend all night at the lighthouse doing his job *and* Lew's job, and all day asleep. Usually he worked for only half the night, and then he'd come home and sleep for a while. Just a while, not all day. There'd been a problem with finding someone to do Lew's job and it had made her parents cross.

Annie couldn't see her father in the day now, so she'd sneak in and watch him sleep instead. It would be dark in the bedroom because there were two layers of curtains to keep the sun out, but if she stood long enough she could see his sticky-up hair against the pillow and hear the snuffles of his breathing. He made her think of a hedgehog.

Thing was, Annie's father always thought of interesting things for her and Robbie to do over the summer: they'd help him paint the door of the lighthouse or collect flotsam on the beach or go on expeditions. But Annie's best sort of expedition was just two of them: her and Dad. It could be anything, really, as long as Robbie didn't come. Walks were good. With sugar sandwiches. She liked the quiet way they did things together. It felt like being wrapped up in a big blanket made of wind and grass and clicking cicadas. When Robbie came, it got noisy and worrying. He always seemed about to fall down steep banks or be chased by a bull.

This summer, Annie had spent a lot of time in the hedge and learning to knit, and Robbie had played commandoes on his own or, now and then, with his friend Tom. Although even on his own, Robbie sounded like a whole army.

Explosives in place, it's about to blow.

Roger that.

K-K-K-Kapow.

Dad was good at commandoes. He'd make lightning raids into the kitchen for sugar sandwiches and rig up complicated tents. Without him, Robbie spent a lot of time blowing up the clothes line, which Annie's mother didn't like because it got dirt on the sheets.

"I miss your dad, too," she said, "but we'll have him back soon, don't you worry. Lew's replacement gets here tomorrow." She stopped looking at the window in a wondering way and looked at Annie instead. "Off you go then and play in the hedge, but don't climb through to the other side. Mr. Gregory moved the bulls into the back paddock yesterday."

"Okay."

"And when you get back, can you play with Robbie for a bit?" Her mother's face had that I-know-I'm-asking-a-lot look. "I've just got the bit around the windows to do..." She was painting the bathroom aqua blue. It was taking forever. "Then we can plant some lettuces if you like."

Annie made a noise like air coming out of a balloon. "Do I have to play with him? He's always so *sticky*."

"Just take him outside for a while—it doesn't have to be commandoes—throw a ball or something."

"A *sticky* ball. Throw a *sticky* ball."

Annie's mother lifted her eyebrows. "Easier to catch?"

Under-over-through-and-off.

With *off*, Annie's body, all of its own accord, slipped out the door, down the steps, into her waiting boots, and across the lawn. She felt like a ball of wool running away under the table but still attached to its needles. She looked back at the cottage while she ran—it was almost the exact same blue as the sky and the reflecting windows, so if she scrunched up her eyes it wasn't there any more. Then she was almost at the hedge, and the house had disappeared completely behind a rose bush. Annie liked that feeling of being the only person around.

Even though her mother couldn't see what she was up to, Annie would still do what she'd been told. Not because there was anything to worry about on the other side (she'd watched Mr. Gregory shift the bulls out of the paddock first thing in the morning), but because the hedge wasn't something to climb through, it was an adventure in itself. Ten small trees in a row—what her mother called *shrubs*—and Annie knew every one of them by name.

There was Russell who rustled even when there wasn't a breeze, Holly who was shy and spiky and tried not to rustle in case she scratched herself, and Sprout who had orange berries the size and shape of Annie's thumb and yelled "hah!" every time a bird took one. Sid and Hog and Manny and Sylvie and George were there too, and, tucked in the middle, Mr. and Mrs. Hedge. They had first names like the others, but since they were the oldest shrubs in the hedge and therefore the most important, they'd asked Annie to call them Mr. and Mrs. Hedge. So she did. They called each other that, except sometimes when there was a particularly beautiful sunset or a new nest of eggs to look after, and then he'd call her Pitty and she'd call him Tup.

So here's Annie at the end of the garden in her garden boots—loppity loppity loppity—and Russell says, "Annie's coming," all airy and rustly, and his leaves shiver and show their pale underneaths. Being on the end of the hedge by the gate, he always rustles more than the other shrubs, especially when there are people and animals about.

"Hi Russell." Annie ran her fingers through his leaves, making him giggle. Holly was nodding "hello," and Annie nodded back and kept her fingers to herself. Pale green leaves with soft edges frilled out of Holly's dark spiky ones; behind them, her eyes shimmered in the gathered dark. Annie wasn't close to Holly in the way she was to the other hedge plants, but one day soon she planned to put on gardening gloves and a cardigan and spend time with her.

Sprout was waving, and his waving dislodged an enormous wood pigeon that flopped past Annie's face—*foomp foomp foomp*—and the other trees waved, too: Sid's red flowers with the yellow tips, George's blue flowers, Sylvie's skinny leaves that flashed silver. Then there was Manny with leaves like pins, and Hog who was busting out all over with skinny branches and water shoots.

In the middle of the row were Mr. and Mrs. Hedge, beckoning for her to come. They had the knobbliest trunks of any of the shrubs and the strongest branches. Once upon a time when the garden had begun, they'd been on their own, just the two of them side by side—Tup's shiny leaves as bright as mirrors reflecting Pitty's wavy leaves on twiggy branches. That's how Mrs. Hedge told it to Annie, anyway—how the two of them stood there looking straight ahead for months, then finally started looking sideways at each other (shyly, as she tells it), and then one day they said their names to each other.

Pitty.

Tup.

After that, seedlings had been planted beside them in a line, one by one, year by year. Sylvie. Hog. George. Sid. Sprout. Holly. Manny. Russell. No plan to it, just shrubs chosen by the lighthouse keeper who lived in the cottage back then. Eventually Tup and Pitty began to lose their edges and become...well, it has to be said, a hedge.

"I prefer hedgerow," Mrs. Hedge said to Annie once. "A *row* of trees—all individual specimens. That's us. Hedge sounds so ordinary."

But look, Mr. and Mrs. Hedge are still beckoning. They have something special to show Annie. They always do.

*

"Be quiet or you'll scare them," said Mrs. Hedge in a "be quiet" sort of voice which was actually quite loud because the cicadas were arguing again—*whose suit? whose suit? whose suit?*—through the hedge. Annie had looked for them as she'd climbed in, but as usual she couldn't see a single one. She wondered if Robbie had thought about cicada camouflage. If he dressed like that, Ma wouldn't be able to spot him out by the clothes line. She'd hear the noises but by the time she turned around it would be too late.

Kapow.

What Annie could see was a raggedy row of ants making its way up one of Mrs. Hedge's branches and down the other side.

"I bet they tickle," said Annie.

"Not really, love," said Mrs. Hedge. "I barely notice them."

Annie had pulled herself on to a lower branch which was as thick as both her legs and both her arms put together, and she was standing now, trying to avoid the sharper branches. As she stood, she turned her head in the direction of Mrs. Hedge's voice and found herself looking straight into a pair of eyes: green like her mother's, but a speckled sort of green that quivered before darting back behind a leafy fringe.

The faces in the hedge weren't like human faces with one shape that stayed that way; they shifted depending on the time of day and what the wind and the sun were doing. And they kept to themselves, looking at people sideways and talking behind a handful of leaves. The quieter Annie was, the more she saw and heard—which suited her just fine. Today, she was being shown the nest.

Annie had watched the fantails build it with grass and sticks and cobwebs, using their beaks for knitting needles and making the same noises her mother made:

rustles and clicks. The nest was a small and perfect circle with a tail underneath, and as neat as a pair of wool socks. When it was ready, she had been allowed to climb up to see the small speckled eggs. Five! Like toes.

Today, they'd hatched.

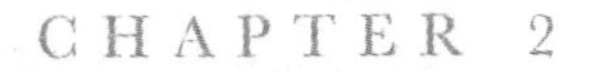

CHAPTER 2

The nest

The hatchlings were difficult to see in the patches of shadow and light inside the hedge. It was the father bird darting in with an insect in his beak that made them spring up so Annie could see them properly. Shc watched the five tiny beaks pop open, greedy and yellow, and shout something that sounded like "pick me!" over and over, as loud and as fast as they could. But the father bird didn't stop to choose. He shoved the squirming insect into the closest beak and left—not flying off in a straight line like other birds, but using his black and white fan to zig-zag through the branches and out over the lawn.

The shouting in the nest died away, leaving only "pick" and "pick" and "pick" and a very quiet "me." By then the cicadas had stopped arguing and were joining in: *pick-pick-pick-meee*, they said, on and on.

Annie moved her hands up the thick branch, which looked rough but was in fact fuzzy like her dad's face when he got home in the morning, and pulled herself closer to the nest. She laid her cheek against the branch and watched. The hatchlings weren't pretty like human babies—they were *ugly*, their eyes covered by eyelids that looked like giant bruises, and they had orangey fluff on their naked heads.

"Where's their mother?" she said.

"Probably gone off to make another nest," said Mrs. Hedge. "It's what fantails do. *I'm* here, though, and I haven't lost a baby bird yet. They're safe with me. I take great care to shelter them from rain and sun, and when the wind comes I hold tight to the nests to stop them falling. Not all shrubs take that trouble."

"Absolutely," said Mr. Hedge. "She hasn't lost a bird yet. People think hedges—"

"—hedgerows—" said Mrs. Hedge.

"*—hedgerows* are here to stop the wide world getting

in and girls getting out, but we're more important than that. We are the place between what is known and what is unknown, we are protection—"

"—and shelter—" said Mrs. Hedge.

"—and shelter, and we're *r-r*-ready, Annie, whatever happens. *R-r-r*-ready for anything." He had a way of saying an *r* that sounded like marbles rolling around inside a jar. Annie caught a glimpse of his mouth. It was big and spiky with thin sticks at all sorts of angles—just like a nest.

"Ready," said Mrs. Hedge firmly, as if she were writing the word down with a very sharp pencil.

"For tigrish," said Mr. Hedge, nodding, "for example."

"Tigers?" said Annie.

"Tigrish," said Mr. Hedge, louder.

Grish-grish-grish, said the cicadas.

"Ti*g*rish," said Annie, laughing, and she let the word roll around in her mouth too. "I like the way you say it, Mr. Hedge, it sounds more exciting than tiger. It sounds as if it's roaring and about to bite."

Mr. Hedge nodded more vigorously this time. "*R-r-r*-roaring," he roared, and his breath smelled like her father after he'd mown the lawn. Annie heard Holly gasp and Sprout say "hah!" and "hah!" again.

"They *are* more exciting than tigers, Annie, and more scary too," said Mr. Hedge. "They do all sorts of things tigers can't do—they're bigger and stronger for a start. They could, if they wanted to, bite a little girl in two with one snap of their jaws—"

"I'm not a little girl," said Annie. "I'm nearly ten years old, which is like *ten shrubs* in a row, and that means I'm not scared of tigers or *tigrish* either." She said it again. "Tigrish."

The cicadas joined in like an echo. Or a spell. *Grish-grish-grish.*

Her mother told her that when she was uncertain about something, she should say the name of the thing out loud to herself to get a better understanding of it. A name has its own magic, she'd say. When you say it the right way, you learn what that magic is.

"I dream about tigers sometimes," Annie said. "Last night, I was in a circus and I held up a flaming hoop for a tiger to fly through."

"Are you sure it was a tiger?" said Mr. Hedge in a low sort of voice that made her feel like she'd done something wrong.

Annie looked at Mr. Hedge. The sun was lighting up his leaves so every vein could be seen. It looked like each leaf held its own miniature tree.

"I ..." Annie stopped. No, she wasn't sure.

"There aren't many girls who aren't afraid of tigrish," said Mrs. Hedge brightly. "Ordinary girls who dream of castles and princes don't have any idea there are tigrish out in the world. Ordinary girls who wake up with bright faces like small suns usually skip right past us and see nothing of interest here. You see all these things, Annie, because you're dappled, like us."

"Dappled?" said Annie.

"Dappled," said Mrs. Hedge, and pointed at Annie's arms.

Annie looked. As far as she could see, her arms were just ordinary arms holding on to Mrs. Hedge's fuzzy gray bark. They were brown from the summer sun and a bit freckly.

"Dappled," she said again slowly. It sounded like "apple," which was funny, and a bit like "dimple," which made her smile. That's when she noticed the patterns on her skin made by sun shining through the shadows of the leaves. Annie held her hands up in front of her face and turned them like ballerinas in a music box. Each time they turned, the patches of sun slid across her skin and settled into different shapes. The more she looked, the more her hands looked like they belonged to someone else.

“Ooh!” said Mrs. Hedge, shaking so hard her leaves clapped, and then Mr. Hedge’s leaves started to clap, and Holly’s clattered and Russell’s rustled, until all the shrubs were at it. For Annie, it was like being in a room of people clapping with gloves on. One by one they stopped until Russell let out a long sigh that became “tigrisssh.”

“Tigrrrish,” said Mr. Hedge, less rustly, more roary. “Not an earthquake at all.”

Annie felt her skin shiver. Tigrish were one thing in dreams or in conversation, quite another thing standing right in front of you. The dappled patterns on her arms had disappeared. There was no sun shining through the leaves any more and the cicadas were silent.

“Where is it?” said Annie.

“He’s gone,” said Mr. Hedge. “Just passing by, that time. He had something to do.”

One of the fantails squeaked a tiny “me.” The hatchlings had their heads on one side, listening intently. One of them, smaller than the rest, its head wobbling on its skinny neck, squeaked again and looked at Annie with blind eyes.

“Shhhh, Bud,” said Mrs. Hedge.

“Bud?” said Annie.

“I call him that, just to myself. He’s so small,

I thought if he had a name he might feel more important, and try harder to eat his insects and grow big. I see the other ones, the way they push him aside."

Bud's little head wobbled again, then he opened his beak and waited. He *was* like a bud, thought Annie, a little hopeful rosebud, and the eyelids were petals waiting to open. Really, the other babies weren't ugly either. All wobbly and hopeful and soft. She wanted to ask Mrs. Hedge if she could hold them. She imagined their skin as thin as tissue paper and the bones underneath like sewing needles. But before she could ask, something else happened.

The sounds in the garden and the paddock and the hedge changed. All at once, in a whoosh, they got louder and then softer, and then there was nothing. It was a deep dark sound like a wave breaking in a cave. It came and it went, and now Annie felt properly scared.

"Is everything all right?" she said.

Mrs. Hedge shivered once from root to tip. "Yes, Annie," she said. "Everything's all right. Are you all right, Bud?"

Bud wobbled a bit and then wobbled again. The other babies wiggled. They made Annie think of Robbie when he was running around with no clothes on before his bath. She wondered if her brother had woken up from his sleep yet and if he'd heard the strange sound and was frightened. She wanted to go home.

"Goodbye, Mrs. Hedge," she said. "Goodbye, Mr. Hedge," and hand over hand she climbed down. One, two, and she was on the ground. The smell of the earth rose up around her as if it had rained. She brushed her hands on her legs, and watched as two insects fell from her sleeve and staggered off into Mrs. Hedge's roots.

They were earwigs—usually so shiny and self-important—but today they hurried. There were insects staggering about in all directions, in fact. The ants had gone.

Annie dropped to her knees to get under a low branch and crawled out on to the grass. It was cool under her hands, but when she looked up, the day was still hot and blue and bright. Annie listened. She listened hard. Still no cicadas.

Crackle. It was Holly.

"I have to get home, Holly."

Cra-a-a-ckle.

Russell was rustling too, but not as he usually did. It sounded like a shiver now. "Shoo," he said. Which meant "see you." Or Annie thought it did.

"Shoo," she said, and tried to smile.

Hog snuffled, and Sprout held out his berries which shone like orange crayons in the sun. Annie noticed some of them were starting to wrinkle in the heat. She nodded goodbye and ran across the lawn as fast as she could go in her boots. Robbie and his honey sandwich made her run. She had to see he was all right.

CHAPTER 3

Robbie

Robbie was standing on a stool in the kitchen, his arms deep in the sink.

"Car wash," he said and held up his tractor covered in bubbles. One bubble was nearly as big as the tractor. It stretched and stretched as big as Robbie's smile and then—"Ye-hah!" he said—it popped.

"You were quick," said Annie's mother, who had changed into her painting overalls and was sitting at the end of the kitchen table with spots of blue paint on her hands. "I've done the first coat." She was watching

Robbie, her eyes half-shut, squinty almost.

It was so bright and normal in the kitchen, Annie had to blink.

Yes, it was. Normal. And smelling of bubbles. No dark noises. No tigrish. Really, it was silly, who'd heard of such a thing?

"Did you hear it?" she said to her mother.

"Mmmm?"

"A kind of roaring noise. I thought it was an earthquake at first."

"Roaring?" said her mother sleepily.

"Like a…oh, it doesn't matter. Robbie's awake."

"Yes he is, and now *I* need to sleep. That earthquake…I barely slept. Robbie kicking all night…" Her eyes were almost closed.

"Is Dad back?"

"No, not yet. I tried to call him, but…" Her mother gave a deep tired sigh. "Oh, he has so much to do with Lew off…" Her eyes snapped shut and looked like they'd never open again. Breathing filled the bright kitchen, the only sound except for Robbie's humming.

"The Wheels on the Bus" was the song he loved best and he hummed it loudly. He was swooshing the tractor through the bubbles in bigger and bigger sweeps, and bubbles were all around the sink and the stool he was standing on, and two were stuck to his hair like a decoration. Then all of a sudden he was wailing. And the wailing grew to a shriek.

"Robbie, shush," said Annie. "Ma's asleep."

"Car wash," he gulped. "The bubbly's going..."

Annie was beside him, shooshing and dipping her hands in the water. She sounded like Mrs. Hedge talking to Bud. "It's the plug—I'll find it." But she couldn't at first, and when she did, it slipped from her fingers and the last of the water was gone in a slurp, leaving only a layer of small bubbles in the sink, winking at them.

"You big *egg!*" said Robbie, and then he shrieked some more, his mouth open as wide as it would go, as wide as a hungry baby bird's. Which made Annie think.

"Would you like to see newborn baby birds? This small?" She held her hand up close to his face, her finger and thumb showing how small. His face was wet with tears and something thickish coming out of his nose. He had their father's striped cooking apron on, and it was damp and bubbly too.

"Let's go outside quietly, then we'll come back—quietly—and tell Ma all about the tiny birds."

Robbie looked at his mother: her eyes shut and her mouth open. Annie waited.

“Tiny, tiny, tiny, birds,” said Robbie in a tiny voice, his thumb and finger opening and shutting like a tiny beak.

“Uh-huh,” said Annie.

“Feed them worms?”

“Oh, okay.”

“O-*kay*!” he said, loudly now, and Annie went “shush” again, and he climbed down off the stool.

“Wipe your face and get another tee-shirt on,” said Annie. “That one’s wet. But be really quick and really quiet like a…” a bubble came away from his hair and floated towards the door as if it had somewhere to go… “like a bubble. I’ll wait for you outside.”

Robbie was quicker than quick. He’d found a tee-shirt, the one that had been his cousin Paddy’s once. It was red and faded and had two holes to put fingers through.

“Good,” said Annie. She’d been standing listening while Robbie was getting ready. There were no more strange roaring sounds outside, and the cicadas were back to arguing. *Zip-it zip-it zip-it*, they said.

Robbie pushed his hand up inside his tee-shirt, poked his fingers through the holes and wiggled them. “This is my worm-hunting shirt,” he said.

“We can do that later,” said Annie, “come on.”

"After the baby birds?"

"Yup."

Robbie followed her down the steps and on to the grass. He was looking at his boots which were old ones of Annie's and a bit too big, so the rubber sloshed about his feet.

"How do worms walk without legs?"

"They don't walk," said Annie.

Robbie looked at her. When he thought about things, his eyes went big and wide and stayed that way. He didn't even blink. She kept walking.

"Wait for me!" said Robbie, but Annie didn't. "Worms *do* walk and they do have legs," he said at last, running beside her, lop-loppity lop-loppity. "And when they do have legs they're called lizards."

"They're not the same thing."

Robbie stopped suddenly and bent to pick something up from the ground. "I know what lizards are, really." He was studying the palm of his hand and whatever it was he'd picked up. "Really, really, really."

Annie kept walking.

"They're cute dinosaurs."

"What? Dinosaurs aren't cute, Robbie. They're huge and ferocious."

She was thinking about the Hedges—would they

mind Robbie coming? Would they talk to him? What if he wasn't *dappled*?

"Well, some dinosaurs are cute," he said. "They're small as chickens and eat grass."

Annie looked down at her little brother. His hair was flattened on one side where he'd been sleeping, and there was something that looked like honey on his cheek and a rim of orange juice around his mouth. He tipped to one side as he walked so he could see things he needed to pick up. On one hand, her brother was loud and sticky and annoying, but on the other hand, he knew interesting things about animals and snuggled up when she read to him. Right now, he was trying hard to be quiet as they approached the hedge, which meant he was making noises that sounded like a cat mewing and trying to take small tip-toey sorts of steps.

"Robbie, cats eat birds. The little birds in the nest might be scared if you meow at them."

"I'm not a cat. I'm a cute dinosaur called David."

Annie made a little beak with her finger and thumb, and tried to pinch Robbie's cheek with it, but he ducked and ran around the rose bush. By the time Annie caught up, he was standing in front of Russell.

"Where's the nest?" said Robbie.

The row of shrubs stood like any row of shrubs would.

Rustling a little, creaking a little, saying nothing.

"Here, I'll show you," said Annie.

"Hatchlings. They're called hatchlings." It was Russell.

"Hatchlings," said Robbie, looking not one bit surprised.

"They're very, very hungry," said Sylvie, and her leaves shimmered in a friendly way.

Robbie smiled at Sylvie. "I'm hungry, too."

"Noisy," said Manny sharply. "Always noisy."

Ferocious-ferocious-ferocious, yelled the cicadas.

"Them, too," said Manny.

"Here, climb up," said Mrs. Hedge, moving a branch to one side. "Nice to meet you, Robbie."

"Nice to meet you, too," said Robbie, climbing in.

Annie followed.

"Ouch, ouch, ouch," said Robbie. "The tree scratched me."

"Take it slowly," said Mr. Hedge, "and we'll move our branches so you won't feel them."

"There," said Annie, pointing. "The baby birds are in the little nest. You have to be quiet or they'll get scared. Be a bubble."

Robbie climbed up so his blue shorts were level with Annie's eyes. She could see his back pocket had bulgy bits where he'd put his little things, what he called his shinies: small stones and bottle tops and dice and Lego bricks and walnut shells. They weren't all shiny, really, but their dad said Robbie was a magpie and magpies liked shiny things, so that's how they came to be called that.

Annie could see the way Mrs. Hedge had cupped her branches around Robbie and was watching him closely. Just a glimpse of her eyes, and then they were gone.

"Bud's the littlest one," said Annie. "The one with the wobbly head."

"Getting bigger," said Mrs. Hedge, "and noisier—listen to that squeaking! They think you've brought worms, Robbie."

"One, two, three, four, five," said Robbie, counting. "There are five baby birds."

"They're hungry," said Mr. Hedge. "Bud especially—he misses out. He's small and the other babies push him aside."

"Worms," said Robbie, and he pushed one hand into his back pocket. Out came a broken rubber band. Robbie wiggled it in front of his nose, sniffed, then pushed it back where it had come from. He fiddled around some more. A cotton reel. String. Then a fat thing that was brown and pinkish. It wriggled.

"Here, Bud," Robbie said, and dropped it into the nest.

All Annie could hear were the cicadas. Then:

"He did eat it!"

"Yes, he did," said Mrs. Hedge. "Thank you, Robbie." And the leaves parted, and there were the leafy eyes. Robbie didn't see them—he was too busy watching the nest.

"In one gulp!" said Robbie.

"I would think so," said Mr. Hedge. "That was a nice fat worm."

"I've got my worm-hunting tee-shirt on," said Robbie, "that's why I found it," and he waved towards the rose bush. "You know, Mrs. Hedge, birds are cute dinosaurs, too."

That's when the leaves around Robbie shivered and shivered. Then they shook and shook. And a sound like a huge wave rushed towards them. Annie tugged hard at one of Robbie's back pockets.

"Let's get down."

Robbie stayed as he was.

Annie tugged again—sharper this time—and the pocket wriggled. A cute something was in there. She let go.

The wave of sound made her feel like she'd jumped

into a pool of icy water—there were goosebumps all over her arms and neck. Whatever it was, it was coming closer, sweeping the wire fence and crashing across the lawn…

Wind. Sending the wire fence twanging, billowing the sheets on the line, pushing and shoving its way between Annie and Robbie and the Hedges, roaring in their faces. Mrs. Hedge's mouth moved but didn't make a sound as she struggled to keep a grip on the nest. Mr. Hedge gripped Mrs. Hedge.

"Robbie," yelled Annie over the torrent of air, "get down!"

He was reaching for the nest with one hand and trying to hang on to a branch with the other.

"No, no, no! Hold on with *both* hands." Annie shouted so hard her voice cracked.

Robbie was saying something over his shoulder, but she couldn't hear a word, she could just see his mouth moving. Everywhere there were leaves and wind and seeds and feathers, whipping and prodding and snapping, and snatching words away.

Annie pulled hard at his shorts again.

"You're. Not…" Robbie turned his head properly so she could see his mouth shouting and his angry wide-open eyes. "The. Boss. Of. Me."

Mrs. Hedge's branches were straining to keep the nest from flying away. One broke near the tip and flapped crazily in Annie's face.

"Let *me* hold the nest," said Annie, ducking and speaking right where she thought Mrs. Hedge's ear was.

Mrs. Hedge shook herself vigorously, and Mr. Hedge shouted, "We haven't lost a bird yet, Annie! We can do it!" But his mouth after he'd spoken looked like a snapped twig.

CHAPTER 4

The wind

Annie was scratched on her arms and her cheek. The branches that were normally so kind to her were hurting now—whipping the air and across her skin. The air was full of leaves and seeds and grasses. One lodged in her eye and made it weep. There was something soft now too. A feather? And an unexpected smell—it was something Annie knew, and it made her feel briefly hopeful, but she couldn't work out what it was. She was stuck holding on to Robbie's pocket, waiting for it all to be over.

A loud tearing noise that sounded like crying—and crying that sounded like something tearing in half—and then Robbie was moving up the branch, both his hands grabbing at branches and leaves. Annie pulled his pocket, and Robbie slipped, thudded into her chest, pushed out all the air…

She held him tight anyway. His hair in her face. And they watched as the little nest, torn from Mrs. Hedge's arms, was carried away. It skimmed over the bull paddock and the wire fence, lifted slightly then continued on towards the sea.

With it went the wind.

It was as still as could be.

Mrs. Hedge was crying. Not a soft, wet sound, but a dry, harsh bark. Her branches heaved and shook and scratched.

Mr. Hedge was breathing as if he'd been running. He patted Mrs. Hedge and leaned in close. "Pitty…" he said.

"Oh, Tup…"

"Will you stop that shaking please?" said George. "The wind was bad enough. Look at the flowers I've lost." In front of him were the petals that made up his big blue flowers. There was one left, as big as a dinner plate, bobbing on the end of a branch. He pulled it close.

"She's upset," said Mr. Hedge, "leave her alone."

"*She's* upset?" said Manny. "We're all upset—and we're upset because she's upset, and we're connected because we are, whether she likes it or not, a *hedge*. I put up with the feeding times of those baby birds of hers, and those stupid cicadas—why she can't tell them to go and argue somewhere else is beyond me—and I wouldn't object to a little *weeping* at a time like this, but this is too much."

"A few flowers here and there are nothing," said Holly, clearing her throat. "I am sorry for your loss, Mrs. Hedge. You were a good mother to those babies."

"Well, if you don't have flowers," muttered Manny, "I don't suppose you'd understand—"

"You are a good mother," said Sprout. "There's no doubt about that." His berries lay scattered and bright on the ground in front of him, and he was leaning forward trying to scoop them into piles.

"My leaves…" Russell said.

"A branch for me," said Sid. "I think it's cracked."

Hog just snuffled.

With that, Mrs. Hedge fell quiet.

Mr. Hedge stood staring out into the world where the nest had gone. Just for a moment, Annie saw his eyes, his nose, his mouth. All of him. He reminded

Annie of the sad giant in a picture book she read to Robbie sometimes. Just then their mother's voice floated into the tangled air, calling them home.

Mr. Hedge ruffled, and his face disappeared. Annie stood perfectly still and did nothing. She felt like a sad giant too.

Robbie wriggled from her arms and was scrabbling away across the grass, ducking to pick things up, calling, "Hereiyam!"

"You must go too," said Mrs. Hedge.

Annie screwed her eyes up tight and tried to screw her ears up too, but Mr. and Mrs. Hedge lifted their branches to give her room to climb out and Mr. Hedge gave a small pat.

The lawn was sprinkled with all the things the wind had left: leaves, dandelion heads, blue petals, orange berries, a branch with red flowers on it. There was a feather, too, a long thin one with dark stripes that she hadn't seen before. Annie was about to pick it up, but her mother called again.

"I'll be back," Annie said over her shoulder, and ran off towards the house.

"Shoo," said Russell.

Out in the field, the bleached paddock grass was standing up again, blade by blade. The wire fence hummed and crackled with the salt brought in from the sea. In the distance, white against a brightening sky, was the lighthouse. There was no sign of a nest.

One cicada after another creaked back to life, and the father fantail returned with a fat green beetle in his beak. He hovered where the nest had been, head darting in all directions, the beetle's legs waving wildly. Then he was off, dipping and diving in the air, the weight of the insect causing him to dip lower than usual. But each time, he bobbed up again, and then he was gone.

CHAPTER 5

Finding your feet

"I've lost the baby birds," said Mrs. Hedge. "I've lost Bud."

Mr. Hedge held out a branch crooked in the middle like an elbow. Mrs. Hedge lifted one of her branches and slid it through his.

"You haven't lost them yet, love," he said.

Mrs. Hedge said nothing. If she spoke, she might cry again. She thought of the father fantail flying bravely after the nest without pausing to decide what to do, without pausing even to drop the wriggling beetle.

One minute he was there and then he was gone. What would it be like to decide something and then to *do* it? A shrub couldn't do a thing. It could only stand and wait.

A small gust of air puffed out Mr. Hedge's chest, and Mrs. Hedge yelped and held tight. She felt her own branches spread like a skirt. Then the wind was gone, and Mr. Hedge was standing beside her like any common-or-garden hedge, except his mouth was trembling.

Mrs. Hedge looked at the paddock. It was a place she knew well but didn't really know at all, and beyond the paddock she knew only what Annie had told her.

"Just because we haven't done something before doesn't mean we can't do it," Mr. Hedge was saying.

The breeze nudged again.

"Humphrey," said Mr. Hedge softly, so softly Mrs. Hedge almost missed it. He only ever said "Humphrey" when he was worried. It was the name of the dog who used to live in the garden and always chose Mr. Hedge's trunk to pee on.

Mr. Hedge had known how to walk for some time, but had never until now actually done it. Not properly. It started when he'd heard Annie telling Robbie a story in the garden about giants that walked and talked. The only giants Mr. Hedge knew were trees—was there anything bigger?—and it had got him thinking. So one night, when the garden was asleep, he'd worked away quietly, clenching and pushing and wriggling at the place where his main trunk met the earth. He'd concentrated all the sunlight he'd stored in the cells of his leaves and all the water in the cells of his trunk until amazingly, *finally*, he'd felt something he'd never felt before or even imagined. His trunk—slowly, squelchingly—separated from its roots.

Mr. Hedge had felt so light and so excited he thought he might float away, but he was terrified, too. Rather than float, what he'd probably do was topple over and become firewood. So he'd clenched and pushed and wriggled until his trunk had meshed with his roots again, and he'd never told Mrs. Hedge about it. Just kept it to himself in case of emergency.

"There's nothing for it," said Mr. Hedge, "we must go and find them."

He heard Russell make encouraging noises behind him, and Manny sniff, and he raised his voice and spoke to the whole hedge.

"Dear friends, I am going to do something now that is rather unexpected. It is not without its dangers but, done correctly, I hope all will be well. I advise you not to try it until you see how I go."

Mrs. Hedge started to speak but Mr. Hedge stopped her. He closed his eyes. Not one of the shrubs rustled or spoke.

Mr. Hedge clenched and pushed and wriggled. It made Mrs. Hedge think of Annie curling up her toes when the garden path was too hot to walk on, but it *sounded* like the gate opening—a deep, woodenish groan. At last, he moved shakily off his roots and Mrs. Hedge saw him stand—*stand!*—on the grass. He reached for one of her branches to steady himself, but she pulled them back close to her trunk. She felt hollow inside, as if an insect had chewed everything up.

Mr. Hedge teetered a little but he didn't fall over. "I didn't tell you, Pitty, because I didn't want you to worry," he said. "You must believe me now: this is one thing shrubs can do. Please. Hold. On. To. Me."

Mrs. Hedge thought of the fantail. Of being free to go anywhere. It was a shock, though, to see Mr. Hedge moving about as if he'd done it all his life. Why hadn't she know about this? Mrs. Hedge didn't know what she knew any more, she didn't know what to think even. But she knew the right thing to *do*, so she held out a branch.

Mr. Hedge took it.

"Thank you, Pitty," he said. "I haven't tried this bit

before but I've been thinking about it for a while." He began to rock.

"Hah!" said Sprout.

"Yes," said Sylvie.

And Mr. Hedge rocked and rocked until his trunk,
with a creak,
divided in two.

"Legs," said Mrs. Hedge with a squeak.

"Legs-egs-egs-egs?" The word echoed down the hedgerow, picked up by one shrub after another.

Mr. Hedge nodded vigorously, his eyes as bright as a bird's. He took hold of one of Mrs. Hedge's branches, and lifted it as if asking her to dance. "Shall we?" he said.

"Ahhhh," said Holly.

"What's all this?" said Manny as if he'd suddenly woken up. "Walking shrubs? How's a hedge to keep itself together? I tell you, if they're going, then I'm going to move out, too. Find myself a space right in the middle of the lawn and plant myself there. A specimen plant, a standard manuka. Now that's got a good sound to it."

Mrs. Hedge smiled a small smile at her husband as if she hadn't heard, then she looked down and set to work. It took her longer than it had taken Mr. Hedge but at last, with an exhausted groan, she parted from her roots.

"Now, start rocking," said Mr. Hedge. "It's okay, I've got you."

"Legs," she said. And the word felt exciting for the first time. Mrs. Hedge started to rock.

Look, Mr. Hedge and Mrs. Hedge are moving at last. First one leg and then the other through the golden waiting air until, free of the dappled earth under the hedge, they stand on the bristling paddock grass.

Behind them was a frenzy of cicadas and plant chatter, but Mrs. Hedge barely heard it. All her thoughts were on the place she'd stepped into. Not only was the grass crunchy, but the air was different. In the hedgerow, the air was cool and rustly. Out here, it was light and fizzy like the warm lemonade Annie brought for picnics. It seemed to spill over everything in a casual, light-hearted way, making the grass and the trees and wire on the fence clearer and brighter.

Mrs. Hedge blinked and looked at Mr. Hedge. He was different, too. For a while, it had been difficult to work out where she ended and he began. Now Mrs. Hedge could see the shape of his trunk and knots she didn't know existed, and the tips of each one of his shiny leaves. She stared until she felt the old cricket who lived in her lower branches scrabble out and scuttle back to the safety of the hedge. A spider flung himself into the air on a thread that shone like wire, and two earwigs ran off, *tic-tic-tic* on the dry grass. Last to go were six breathless cicadas.

At last they were on their own. Mr. Hedge looked at his wife, and she wondered what he was seeing. She felt flustered without baby birds or insects or other shrubs nearby, and stood flapping her branches, causing a flurry of silver as the leaves flashed in the light. Never before had she seen herself as a shrub that sparkled.

"Look at us both," said Mr. Hedge. "We're like a pair of Christmas trees, all lit up and nervous. Next we'll be wanting lights and a star."

Hearing his lovely voice with the long rolling *r* stopped Mrs. Hedge from flapping. She gave a shimmery smile instead.

Mr. Hedge smoothed himself down, crooked one of his branches and held it out to her. "Shall we?"

CHAPTER 6

The tigrish

Annie ran out of the house and over the lawn, and straight away saw the gaps in the hedge—people-shaped gaps, as if someone had clipped the shapes of a man and a woman from the knitted branches and taken them away. She could see through to the other side now. There was the blond grass of the paddock, the hill, the dark smudge of the woods and, off in the distance, but not as far as she'd thought, the lighthouse and the blue of the sea. All of these things, so safely far away, were not so distant any more. The people-shaped gaps opened their empty arms and said, "We're not here to stop you. Come in."

Annie smelled the earthy cow smell of the paddock and heard the faint metallic clankings of the lighthouse. She could even feel the sea sucking at the land and spitting it back. These sensations were edging inside her and there were two holes to greet them where once she'd had a head full of branches and leaves.

"Annie..." It was Russell. He spoke so softly, she could hardly hear him. Something about leaves and eggs. No, he was talking about *legs*. Over and over. But as Annie approached, he went silent. His leaves shifted and there were his eyes, the darkest green they'd ever been. Almost black. "It's too late—Mr. and Mrs. Hedge have gone. They're looking for Bud."

"Gone?" said Annie. "But how...?"

"Legs."

"Legs!" said Manny. "If shrubs were meant to have legs they'd have had them from the start."

"Cicadas don't fly from the start," said Russell. "They start out underground, the wings come later."

"I wish I could fly," said Sylvie. "Or walk."

Crackle, said Holly.

Annie thought of the naked, bobbing heads of the baby birds and felt afraid. Afraid for them, and afraid for herself, too, because there were holes in the hedge, and things she didn't know about yet could creep in and find her and her mother and father and Robbie. Annie felt like a boot sitting by the back door waiting for a foot. She had no idea what to do next.

I haven't lost one yet. Mrs. Hedge's voice came from somewhere deep inside Annie's chest.

She closed her eyes so she could hear it better. The cicadas were quieter than usual—*click-click-click* like fingers keeping time—so the words in her head sounded strong and clear. *The thing is, Annie, never to stop watching. To always be alert. When danger comes, we are ready.*

Then came the rolling boom of Mr. Hedge: *Mrs. Hedge is always ready.* And "ready" rolled through Annie's head and filled her eyes up to their lids and squeezed out on to her cheeks. Tickling. Something was tickling.

Her eyes snapped open. Looking at her directly in the face, so close Annie could feel whiskers, so close it filled all the space in front of her, was the tigrish. Annie's eyes brimmed with tears and the powerful face swam, and because it was swimming like that, even though she could feel the whiskers and smell the wet salty breath, she believed she'd dreamed it up. So she didn't scream or run away.

What was in front of Annie looked just like the tiger she dreamed about at night. It had the black markings, the orange fur, the huge paws, the ears. But the night tigers weren't solid like this. They came and went like birds; they didn't smell of anything.

"Tigrish," she said carefully, and waited for the name to speak its magic.

Immediately, she began to feel warmer on her legs. Like standing right in front of an open fire. She thought of the bonfire her father lit in winter, bright and crackling and spitting with heat, and her father's orange smiling face as he threw on armfuls of leaves and branches he'd trimmed from the trees. Was this what the name was telling her? And what did it mean? She wasn't sure if the tigrish was comforting or dangerous—a bonfire could be both.

Annie frowned.

The tigrish crouched down low and looked straight at her, and his eyes were like the sea on a cold day. Yes, *his.* Annie could see that now. How huge he was, his eyes endless and without edges, like the sea from the lighthouse windows. His fur glowing. Annie thought if she touched the tips with her fingers, they would burn.

What was he telling her? She knew.

Climb on.

And if she didn't? What then?

Annie's mother had told her many times not to go through the hedge to the other side without asking first. On the other hand—and here Annie found herself looking from one hand to the other—she'd also told Annie to look after her friends. She called it "loyalty," which sounded like "royalty" and therefore must be grand and important. Was it more important than the rule about going through the hedge? Annie didn't know the answer to that. She turned her hands over and looked at her palms. She named the left one "Don't go through the hedge" and the right one "Loyalty to friends (especially hedges)."

It seemed to her that the rule about the hedge was like "Don't wear your boots inside." It was important but it wasn't unbreakable. If you hurt yourself in the garden, for example, you could run inside with your boots on without being told off. The other one, about friends, was different. It felt like a rule you couldn't break without terrible things happening.

Annie opened and shut her hands, and then opened them again as flat as they'd go, hoping they'd give her a clue what to do. But there was nothing there except a patch of honey on her right thumb. How did that get there?

Annie heard the tigrish make a long, low sound halfway between a moan and a song. *Hurry.*

That's when Annie properly noticed the smell. It was a bit like the smell of the paddocks, like sheep and cows, but it was also the smell of the sea in summer. A kind of salty sweetness. Annie sniffed hard and licked her lips to see if she could *taste* the smell, like you could taste fire when it blew its smoke at you. There was a something there and it reminded her of the drawer in the kitchen where her father kept his special treats. Something *in* the drawer…

Licorice! That's what it was! The tigrish smelled of licorice.

At that moment, one of the fingers of sunlight that had been making its way across the lawn through the gap in the hedge slid across the fingers of one of Annie's hands. It was the one with the honey thumb.

"Loyalty royalty, then," said Annie loudly, and then again: "Loyalty." And she bowed towards the tigrish as if he were a king and she a visiting princess, and she closed her hand on the sunlight to keep it in case she needed it later. This was something her father had taught her to do. Being a lighthouse keeper, he had a lot to say about light.

Annie noticed the fur of the tigrish was shimmering now, blue and gold like the very hottest part of a fire.

"I'm ready," she said.

CHAPTER 7

Through the hedge

"I'm ready," she said again, which meant she wasn't really ready but was trying to be. Annie often told herself things out loud so she would believe them. The thought of jumping on the back of a tigrish and riding out through the hedge was like running too fast down a hill knowing she could trip any minute and roll head-over-heels the rest of the way.

Annie thought of the birds and Mr. and Mrs. Hedge. "I'm ready," she said one more time, and the tigrish looked at her without blinking. His eyes were like the sea after a storm now, each one concentrated at a single bright point. "You want me to hurry?"

The tigrish lowered his head, then lay down in front of Annie like a carpet. From deep inside the dappled fur came another low singing moan.

Annie held her hands over his back without touching the fur and looked at them. "Loyalty to friends" and "Don't go through the hedge" side by side. Her hands were warm but not burning. Slowly she lowered them.

The fur was softer than she'd expected. She could hardly see her fingers, but she could certainly feel them. They were tingling.

Annie lifted a leg over the glowing back and sat herself there, leaning forward to grip the thicket of fur between the shoulders. She could feel the warmth of thc tigrish, and the rumbling inside his body, and the smell of licorice was all over and around her.

Lop-loppity.

What was—?

Thud-ump.

There was a surge of power that made Annie almost let go. She was moving and something was pushing up hard against her back. Her knees holding tight, she twisted her fingers in the fur so she wouldn't slip and tried to look around.

Then there was another little cry, and she felt the hands grip tighter again. She looked at them. Robbie's knuckles were white. One of his pinky fingers uncurled and waved in the air like a fat worm, then curled up again.

Landing on the other side of the fence, there was no heaviness or jolting—the tigrish just seemed to glide into the grass, and the grass let him in.

Annie leaned over to see, and when she did, she tipped slightly and her hands slipped, and Robbie gripped, and she had to sit up quickly to keep balance. She held more tightly to the fur. That's funny, she thought, is it softer? It was thicker around the shoulders anyway, but now it was as if her hands were sinking into a feather quilt. She stared at the golden back with the slashes of black across it like black crayon, and the way the fur fell away in long sweeps, flaring out on either side of the powerful shoulders like...she cried out. Wings! The tigrish had wings!

The great creature tensed its muscles and released them, and two enormous dappled wings—muscle by muscle, feather by feather—unfolded. Then the tigrish leapt forward—no, *lifted off* into the afternoon.

"Fly-ing!" yelled Robbie. He sounded excited now.

Annie shut her eyes. She could feel the air rushing

past and around her like the windy days when she walked the hills with her dad. And she could feel the muscles of the tigrish tense and release each time the wings lifted and fell. Such a strong wide back.

Flying! Was there anything else like it? Slowly, she opened each eye.

CHAPTER 8

Taking to the air

Beneath them, the grass on the hill was dark with shadow and pushed flat. A rabbit froze, its fur flattened too. Annie turned to look behind and saw the grass standing up again and shaking itself and, running through it, like a small flame, the white of the rabbit's tail. It was heading for the hedge and the gap that led into the garden. There was something white waiting for it—a sheet she'd helped her mother peg on the line that morning.

Suddenly Annie was Annie again, not a girl on an

adventure, but a girl who used to help hang out washing and fold it when it was dry. She wondered if her mother would come soon to take the washing in and, if she did, would she call out to Annie and Robbie, thinking they were playing in the hedge? Would she notice the gaps where Mr. and Mrs. Hedge had been?

Thinking of her mother caused a faint roar in Annie's chest.

"Loyalty," she said, looking at her right hand gripping the tigrish fur and the teaspoon of sunshine she'd kept for later. She was being loyal to the Hedges, but what about Ma? She deserved loyalty, too. And there was the complication of Robbie—he was younger than Annie, and her mother would worry a lot more about where he'd gone. She'd say it was Annie's fault. But it wasn't—not really. He'd just *come.*

Could she have stopped the tigrish and told Robbie to get off? Or pushed him off on to the grass? Annie thought back to Robbie playing at the sink with his tractor. She should have found the plug and filled up the sink again, not taken him out to the hedge. If he hadn't come, she might have been able to grab the nest and hold on to it. He was too young for adventures like this, and now she had to look after him. There was no one else. Annie could feel the dampness on the back of her top where Robbie was leaning. He was heavy for a small boy.

Annie let her face drop into the reassuring thicket of fur in front of her. How did anybody know the right thing to do *ever*?

"It's okay, Robbie," she said into the fur. "I'll look after you." She hoped he'd heard, but she couldn't be sure.

Why didn't she sit up and say it?

Because then everyone would hear.

Everyone?

The tigrish.

Annie realized, with her face deep in the tigrish fur, that she could see glimpses of tigrish skin. Was it... could it possibly have stripes as well? She pushed into the fur with her fingertips and parted it so she could see properly.

Yes, the skin was golden with black stripes. It made Annie think of her arms in the hedge, all stripy and not feeling like hers. So the tigrish was dappled too, she thought. *All the time.*

They began to slow.

Annie sat up a bit and felt Robbie do the same. They'd reached the top of the hill. Off in the distance they could see the beach, the rocks, the lighthouse and, at the bottom of the hill, a patch of pine trees they called the Giant Woods because it was like the place in Robbie's story.

The tigrish seemed to stop in the air and hang there before hurtling down the hill towards the lighthouse. But first there were the woods to cross, the woods where Annie and Robbie weren't allowed to go on their own, ever. They'd been there with their dad once on an adventure and hadn't wanted to go back. It was dark and damp, and there were emerald insects and white frilly mushrooms they couldn't eat. Now, as they flew near the first tall tree, Annie could feel the air cool slightly. Then, just as the tigrish's muscles bunched to push himself up and over it, Robbie slipped.

His hands came apart at her waist and grabbed at her top and then her arm, and he was pulling too hard, and pinching the skin, and slipping and—

"Annie!" he howled.

She felt his right hand let go, and then his left. She reached back to grab something—anything—an elbow, some hair…

"Robbie's falling!" she screamed. "Please—"

She felt the tigrish check itself, slow a little, and then start to spiral downwards instead of up. Annie turned her head enough to see Robbie hanging on to the tigrish fur, his legs out behind him, dangling over the tail. His eyes were open as wide as they could go and his face was so white his freckles stood out like stars.

"Annie…" squeaked Robbie in a tiny, tiny voice like a meow, but a real meow, not a made-up one. Then his mouth was opening and shutting, and nothing was coming out.

Annie edged towards him, hanging on to fur in big handfuls. Her whole body felt like it was running on electricity—all shivery and strong. In front of her, Robbie, with his dear white mewing face and his thousand freckles…

"Hold on," yelled Annie, and her voice was a roar, not kind at all. "I'm com-*ing*." And then again, kinder. "You can do it, darling. Hold. Tight."

But he didn't hold tight. He didn't. His little hands, which were good at picking up small things, couldn't hold on to a big hank of tigrish fur any more. Annie saw one hand fly out from his body like a small white bird, then the other, and then all of him p-e-e-l away from the huge stripy back and—*whoosh*—he was gone.

She let go, too. Opened her hands. Flew briefly. And then fell.

CHAPTER 9

The Giant Woods

Into a hedge. Or something like a hedge. There was a nest of branches and vines and dark green leaves. First Robbie, then Annie.

Crash.

Cra-a-sh.

A yelp from the hedge. From Robbie too. Then:

Robbie: "Ouch, ouch, *ouch*."

Annie: "Oooh, *ow*."

They hadn't fallen far. The tigrish had flown lower than Annie realized. Robbie had leaves in his hair and a scratch on his arm, and when he saw the blood he started to cry—big globby tears that wouldn't stop. Annie wanted to cry, but she knew she mustn't. She pulled a branch out of her hair and patted the scratches on her leg.

"There, all better," she said, just like her mother did. And like her dad: "Well, that was an adventure!"

Robbie stopped crying. "Adventure?"

"Yes," said Annie. "That's it."

Robbie looked behind him as if he'd heard something, and then he looked up. The trees were very tall, so his head was tilted right back. It was darker here than the hedge, much darker; the dappled light was more like dappled *dark*, with only freckles of light sprinkled on Robbie's hair and shoulders. It was cooler, too. No cicadas. Annie saw her brother shiver.

She licked her finger and went over to wipe the blood off his arm, but Robbie pulled away. He looked at the fingers on one of his own hands, picked one, licked it and wiped it across the blood, then licked another finger and did it again. He looked up at the trees.

"Where's the tiger?"

"It's not a tiger, Robbie, it's a tigrish. It won't hurt us. It flies. It's magic."

"It does hurt," said Robbie. "It dropped me. It's a big stripy *egg*."

"You're okay, though, aren't you? And look, it gave you another hole."

Robbie looked at his tee-shirt for a moment, then slid his hand underneath it and wiggled three fingers at Annie. "I'm hungry."

Annie thought of the honey sandwich. How long ago had he eaten? It seemed days ago but must only have been a couple of hours. She tried to add it up, but it was too dark here to tell and too much had happened. Was it time for afternoon tea?

"I don't have anything you can eat," she said, "not now. You'll have to wait."

Robbie's face screwed up tight and his jaw pushed out. Annie could tell he was grumpy, which meant he'd do grumpy things like shout and run around like a crazy rabbit. At home, she'd go outside and leave him to it, but she couldn't leave him here.

Everything her brother did was big and loud. The only small things about him were the shinies in his pockets. She liked it when he took them all out and lined them up, because that's when he'd be quiet for a while and she liked hearing the stories he'd tell about each one: where he'd found it, who might have left it there. He had buttons and nails and dice from board games. He had seeds from flowers and the cut-off bits from people's fingernails.

"Robbie, I need your help to get out of the Giant Woods. We need to go and rescue Bud."

"Bud."

"I know you're hungry, but he's hungry, too, and he's really small and really lost. And all his sisters and brothers are hungry and lost. You can help them because you're so good at finding little things. I bet you can find the nest. It won't take long if we hurry, then we can eat."

Robbie's jaw relaxed and he nodded. "I can find it." But he wasn't looking at Annie now. Already his eyes were on something else. He walked over to one of the trees, picked at the bark, looked at the tips of his fingers, licked whatever was there, and then pushed it into one of his front pockets.

"What was that? You can't just lick things—they might be poisonous."

"I'm foraging," said Robbie.

"You're—"

"It's what dinosaurs do."

"Show me."

"A cicada," he said, and tugged at his pocket again. He held out the little brown shell so Annie could see. It was what a cicada left behind when it climbed out of the ground ready to fly off and argue all summer

to tell in the freckled darkness. Each tree with its dark branches was dark in the interior, too.

Annie shivered. It was cold here.

And there was whispering.

Not in a nice way.

A creak. A plopping sound—something falling.

It was like hearing people talking about you, and it made the back of Annie's neck all goosebumpy.

She walked quickly after Robbie—running to catch up. He was fast for a little boy. Annie wasn't sure they were going in the right direction but she followed him anyway, and she liked the way their boots swishing through the pine needles blocked out the whispering.

Then he stopped. Stock still in the path, his feet wide apart. In front of him, a fallen tree.

Reaching out, he touched a baby fern growing from the tree bark. The bark was rough and brown, but the ferns were bright green like lettuce. There were lots of them. They made Annie think of something. Robbie tore off one of the smallest ferns and tucked it in his pocket.

"This is near the stream!" Annie said. "The one where Dad took us to catch tadpoles. Remember?"

"Uh-huh," said Robbie. And he stood still, thinking for a bit, then, "I know!" he shouted, and he ran for the fallen tree and started climbing it. The trunk was huge, so it was a bit of work, but Annie didn't say anything. She knew he'd manage it. Robbie was good at climbing. At the top at last, he stood and waved down at her. She waved back, and one of the pine trees beside the path waved too, its branches swooping just above Robbie's head, then swinging back up again.

There was no wind.

They were the only branches waving in the whole of the Giant Woods, and this time one of them came close to Robbie, and closer...until...

"Duck!" said Annie.

"Where...?"

It was too late. The branch hit Robbie hard on the shoulder, and—*thwack*—again. He staggered.

"Stop it!" cried Annie at the tree. "Stop. It!"

The branch swung again—*thwack*—and Robbie was no longer on the top of the log.

A howl from the other side floated up and over. Then silence.

"Robbie?" Annie was pushing under one of the branches to get to the trunk of the tree, and then grabbing at another branch to pull herself up...and the bark scratched her and the ferns tickled...she took so much longer than Robbie...and she called again but nothing...nothing...

At last Annie reached the top of the log, but before she could see over, she heard a quavery voice make its way through the branches.

"I think it broke…"

CHAPTER 10

The shinies

Annie scrambled down the other side of the log—fell down it, really—until she dropped to the ground beside her brother. He was sprawled flat on his stomach.

"Are you okay? Are you bleeding? What hurts?" Annie tried to think what her mother had done with Lew when they brought him back from the lighthouse with his broken leg. She needed bandages, water…

"I want Mama," said Robbie.

I want her too, thought Annie. But she said, "It's all right, Robbie. I know what to do."

There was something on the ground in front of him—lots of somethings. Annie leaned closer. The shinies.

"Here," Robbie said, holding up his hand. His palm was brown with dirt after all the falling and climbing, and on it were fragments of what must have been the tiniest bird's egg ever. He held it up and didn't move.

"A bird's egg?" said Annie. "Oh, I thought you'd..."

Robbie rolled on to his back and stared up at Annie with his sad face. It really was a sad face with its turned-down mouth and turned-down eyes. She looked at the treasures all jumbled together: a white Lego block, a pebble, a rolled-up piece of red wool, three bottle tops, a leaf...

"Robbie, you've got peppermints!"

"Mmm." He didn't move. "Lew gave them to me."

"Here, look—there must be—"Annie knelt down and picked them up one by one— "Six! And peanuts—*four* of those—and one of Grandma's toffees...Robbie! Did she know you took that? You know, you are a very good finder—we won't be hungry now."

Robbie's face stopped being a picture of sadness. It wasn't happy, but the mouth wasn't turned down, and his eyes looked softer, even sparky. Then he sat up—*boing*—like a spring.

"I am a good finder," he said, and he picked through what was on the ground to see if there was any more to eat. "Apple seed?" he said, holding it up.

"You have that," said Annie.

Robbie put the seed in his mouth and chewed for three chews, then swallowed. "Will I turn into an apple tree?"

"Maybe."

"I will grow only green apples," he said, "and green frogs, and cute green lizards can live on me and eat my green apples."

"Good idea."

Robbie was looking at his feet. "I can feel roots growing. You can pick my first apple, Annie."

"Thanks. That's…are you sure?"

"Yup."

"Thank you, Rob."

"That's okay. And Mama can have the rest for apple crumble." He was humming now and scooping things back into his pockets, then he put out his hand for the peppermints and the peanuts.

Annie gave them to him.

"One for me—" he put a peppermint in his mouth—"and one for you."

Annie was more hungry than she realized. The

peppermint was sweet and zingy. She sucked and, while she sucked, she watched the trees carefully. There were no more waving branches, but she could feel them watching her too. She swallowed. Robbie gave her another peppermint.

While she chewed, Annie leaned close to his ear and spoke quietly. "Did you see the stream when you were up on the log? If we can find it, we'll get away from these trees. I don't like them."

"I saw water over there, like a frog stream or something." He was whispering in the sort of whisper that made lots of spit. Annie wiped her cheek.

"When we've finished eating," she said, "we'll go." She ate a peanut.

It didn't take long to eat everything except the toffee.

"You have it," said Annie.

"Okay," said Robbie.

"We're going now," said Annie loudly to the trees. "I hope you're happy. We have friends who are trees—kind shrubs who look after us. You're not like them."

"I don't like you," said Robbie, standing with one fist in the air, facing a pine tree. "Don't push me over again or I'll get my dad to *chop* you up and put you on the bonfire."

Annie was sure she heard a groan, but her brother

didn't seem to hear anything. He was doing karate chops and yelling, "Ye-hah! Ye-hah! Ye-hah!"

They set off then, in the direction Robbie pointed, and as they walked Annie heard the whispering again. And a creak. And another groan. Big sounds like a tree about to topple. She thought about a night in winter when her mother had taken her outside to see the stars. It was late, but there were so many stars it didn't feel dark at all. They'd stared into the glistening sky until the tips of their ears were numb. It was like she and her mother had dissolved and left behind a constellation: two stars for her, one for her mother, and one in the middle where they held hands. After that, Annie hadn't felt scared of the night at all.

Here was different. It was *dark* dark in places, without even a glimmer of lightness, and the dappled light that flickered over them both felt weak, as if it had fought its way down through the pine trees and had no strength left. That meant Annie kept looking—over her shoulder and off to the sides, her arms prickling, thinking she heard something, saw something…

"Mushrooms!" Robbie shouted and dropped to his knees. Everything in his pockets seemed to rattle together.

"We can't eat those," said Annie, up beside him in an instant. "They're poisonous. Dad said."

The mushrooms were white and frilly like flowers. They were so white, in fact, they looked as if they were lit by something. Robbie put his hand out to touch them. Small greenish insects hovered around him and in front of Annie. There was a smell like wet towels.

"No! Don't touch, Robbie, they're *poisonous*." Annie flapped her hand in front of her face to chase the insects away. She felt their tiny bodies against her palm.

"Okay," he said, and he was up walking again. Just like that.

Annie stared after her brother. And then she smiled. *It's all right, Robbie*, she said to herself, *I know what to do*. Sometimes saying things out loud did make them happen. He'd stopped and was waiting for her, so she ran to catch up.

It didn't take long to leave the insects and the mushrooms and the wet towel smell behind, and for a moment, just a moment, Annie enjoyed the freshness of the wooded air around them and the smell of the pine needles. There was a little more light coming through the trees, and Robbie was humming to himself, and Annie started humming too, and something else was rattling and humming...and suddenly there were branches. Low and close, waving—prodding—pushing them—pushing between them...

"I can't move," said Robbie in a cross voice.

Something hit her hard on the shoulder. Bounced in front of her. Once, twice. Then another one. Pinecones. Through the fallen branch, she saw a pinecone the size of a grenade hit Robbie right between his shoulder blades.

"Stop that!"

"It's not me, Robbie. We have to get out of here."

He had his angry face on—crunched-up eyes and mouth.

"Now!" she said, pushing one of the branches out of the way so she could see him better. She heard something break…had the branch…?

There was a groan, she was sure of it.

"We have to move."

"You're not the boss of—"Another pinecone fell. And another and another. They were coming so fast now it was hard to think. Robbie folded his arms over his head and hunched down, like in an earthquake. Annie did the same. She felt them on her arms, bouncing off the bones in her elbows. Her shoulders. Her back. They didn't stop.

"Push your way out!" she called, and they both charged at the branches and pushed and shoved, but the branches were knitted tightly around them. It was like being in a giant shirt without arm or head holes. Robbie was throwing his whole body around and bouncing back again, yelling, "Hi-yah! Ye-hah!"

"Hi-yah!" Annie yelled. "Ye-hah!"

Robbie was staring at her. He had pine needles in his hair and mud on his cheeks, and his tee-shirt was nearly brown now, not red, and had four holes in it. His eyes were bright. Even in the *dark* dark Annie could see them shining. He lifted his right hand and gave her a long slow salute.

Of course. Why hadn't she thought of it before? "Commandoes!" she yelled. "Drop and crawl!"

Robbie dropped and crawled as fast as a boy could, under the branches and away. Annie dropped, too, and followed the blue shorts. Her nose was almost touching the pine needles, and the low branches of the pine trees were getting caught in her hair, tugging.

"Let go of me!" she screamed, and batted them away. It helped to think like a lizard—flatter, that was better, her arms out either side. Scuttling as fast as she—

Where had Robbie gone? Annie couldn't see anything but pine needles and branches and darkness. There was a chill now across her shoulders and up the back of her neck. Where was he?

She was about to call out when something blue wriggled out from behind a log like a giant beetle.

"Ye-hah!" said the beetle.

"Ye-hah!" said Annie.

Her brother wriggled off, and she followed.

What do people *do* without brothers, she thought. Where do all those feelings go? Like now, this feeling of knowing those blue shorts and the little boy in them more than anything else in this strange place—more than anything else in the whole wide world, in fact—and caring more about him than *all* those things and *all* those people. How did that happen? Especially when most of the time he was so sticky and annoying?

Another branch yanked at Annie's hair. "Yah!" she yelled, and karate-chopped it with both hands. Released, she scrabbled forward—her head as low as it would go—hating every single pine needle and every single pinecone and every scratchy branch and buzzy skidding insect.

She would have to stand up soon. It was horrible being so low to the ground, she almost couldn't breathe…

But wait. Robbie was getting to his feet.

CHAPTER 11

Escape

They were in a clearing. A skinny stream hummed with insects, and boulders were crusty with lichen. There were patches of thistles and other prickly-looking plants. No trees here except for the ones that circled the clearing, and the freckles of light joined up at last into pools of light.

Annie picked a bit of twig out of her hair and brushed herself down with both hands, then brushed again. The pine needles were sticky.

She could feel bruises on her arms.

Robbie hadn't bothered brushing off the pine needles. He was running towards the stream. "Can we drink it?"

"Wait. Let me look," said Annie. It was smaller than she remembered, and greenish with weed and not flowing very fast. She didn't know what she was looking for exactly, but she remembered her dad scooping some up in his hat for her to drink. The taste of it. He said it came down straight off the hills so it was safe. "Yes… I think we can."

"And eat the weed?" said Robbie, slurping the water up to his mouth with his hand.

"Not sure," said Annie.

He picked up a bit and sucked. "You try," he said and threw it.

Annie felt the weed land—*splat*—on her leg. She grabbed it and flung it back. They both watched as the greenish lump faltered in the air and dropped on to one of the rocks.

"Hah!" said Robbie. "Missed!" And he grabbed another dripping handful. Annie moved to one side, but it landed on her anyway. Her arm this time. She was ready. A bigger, higher throw, and the green lump of weed landed right in the middle of her brother's holey muddy once-red worm-hunting tee-shirt.

Robbie poked it. "Squelchy," he said, and picked up another handful. Annie ducked behind a rock. He didn't throw it, though; instead, he rubbed it carefully on to the front of his tee-shirt, then another handful on to his cheeks and chin.

"Camouflage!" Robbie said, and started to laugh.

Annie laughed, too, and it quickly became that hard-to-stop sort of laugh that grows in your stomach and gets so big it aches. Every time she tried to say something, a chunk of laughter pushed its way out of her throat and sent the words back where they'd come from. Robbie didn't even try to speak; he was clutching his stomach, tears streaming down his cheeks and mixing with the water weed.

"Camouflage!" Annie cried out at last, and nearly toppled over with laughter. It seemed like the perfect, most ridiculous word to describe her ridiculous brother. Her cheeks were wet and her throat ached.

Robbie was doubled over and gasping like a freshly caught fish.

"Camou—" he started, but…

…that sound, deep and moaning—like a wave in a dark cave—washed into the clearing and landed there…

"Quick, we have to go."

"What is it?" Robbie had jumped up and was

coming over to her, walking as quickly as he could without running, weed stuck to the corner of his mouth.

"I don't know. But remember when the baby birds were taken away—it's the same..."

Annie knew they had to leave, and right then, but how? She looked around the clearing and back again the other way. Which way had their dad taken them? Looking around and around and feeling scared wasn't any good, it just made her dizzy. Annie blinked, and tried again...turning slowly and letting her eyes stop where there seemed to be a path. Was there a way out? Was it safe?

Something...

Yes...*Something* was coming.

Annie could feel the air being nudged aside to make way for this thing, whatever it was. The clearing didn't feel so big or so safe any more. Robbie was close beside her, dropping down quickly to the ground and pushing whatever he'd found into a pocket. Then he reached out without looking and held her hand.

Just like that, thought Annie. One minute he was Fearless Commando and the next Sticky Little Brother. The hand was certainly warm and sticky, but then so was Annie's. She squeezed it.

A shadow blocked the sun, and Annie and Robbie

looked up. The tigrish. Floating, dipping, curling downwards, he settled into the clearing, his fur brighter than it had ever been. He'd brought the sun with him.

Annie stepped forward.

"No," said Robbie, letting go of her hand. "He'll drop me."

"I'll put you on the front this time," said Annie. "You just have to hang on to the fur on the shoulders and I'll hang on to you."

"No. Not. *Never*."

"Robbie, it's our only way out. I don't know another way, and there's something…" She tilted her head and listened. It was still there, outside the warm lit clearing. "We'll be stuck here, and the trees…the trees are…"

There it was again, a creak—long and loud—and then the sound of a tree crashing to the ground.

"I can find the way," said Robbie, looking over his shoulder, his feet wide apart, his hands clenched. "I'm good at finding."

"Yes, but what about the trees?" Annie was whispering now. "They're mean, really mean, they don't want us to leave. And even if you get past them and find your way out, it will take time. Remember little Bud? He needs your help *now*."

Robbie looked like he was chewing a peppermint.

Had he found another one? He stared at the tigrish and the tigrish looked back at him, his head low to the ground, his ears alert but his eyes soft.

Robbie chewed and looked at his feet. Annie could see he was doing what she did. Looking at each foot, thinking, *go, don't go, go, don't go, go*...wiggle.

The tigrish made that sound he made—the moan that was like a song. Robbie looked up and relaxed one fist and then the other. He stopped chewing. There was another crash among the trees, closer this time, and without saying a word he walked to the tigrish and, a ripple of muscle and goldenness, the tigrish lowered his whole body to help him climb on.

With Robbie settled, the tigrish looked at Annie and bowed his head. When he lifted it again, she looked him in the eye—this time the just-blue of an early summer's morning—and she was saying, You can't drop us this time, and he was saying, I won't. Just like that, without a word spoken. Then she walked over and climbed up behind her brother. Her arms went around him, tightly.

Silent, the Giant Woods with the leaning trees and long dark branches. Silent, the tigrish as he pushed off, spread his beautiful wings and flew. Silent, the children on that broad back, holding on, holding on, holding on.

CHAPTER 12

A hedge can fly

It didn't take long to fly from the Giant Woods to the beach. Within minutes, the sea was so close Annie could see necklaces of seaweed floating and a flash of silver that could have been a shoal of fish. She pointed so Robbie could see them too.

Something else flashed now, hard and bright like a slap. It struck Annie full in the face. She flung both her hands up to block the terrible glare and heard Robbie yowl. Grabbing at his shirt again, she buried her face in his hair and blinked hard. Shreds of shadow drifted in front of her eyes, as if something had shaken loose in her head. The glare had come from the lighthouse. The sun on the huge diamond-shaped windows.

Annie tried again. She looked up carefully, her eyes half-shut and squinty.

The strange thing, she realized, was she could see right inside the windows to the glass lenses that surrounded the lighthouse lamp. They were the oblongs of glass layered like fish scales to make the light appear bigger and stronger—and usually the curtains were shut to stop the sun shining through them and starting a fire. Her dad pulled them every morning. Not today. Today the curtains were open. Annie could see everything.

Was someone moving up there behind the bright windows? Their father? Or were her eyes still creating shadows of their own? She blinked and blinked.

Nothing now.

Maybe it was window-cleaning day—the curtains had to be pulled back for that. Annie liked to help, polishing with handfuls of damp paper until her arms were sore. Sometimes she was allowed to step inside the big dome of lenses to polish them too. It was a magic glass cave that shone small rainbows on her skin.

A movement snagged at the edge of her vision.

On the beach.

But the tigrish wasn't going towards the beach. His huge body had swung towards the lighthouse, and salty air from the sea surged up and over Annie and her brother. It had the same smell as her father's clothes when he walked into the kitchen in the morning and started rummaging in his pockets for treasure. Once he'd found a tiny music box on the beach that still worked when you wound it up.

The tigrish was curling down through the air, readying himself to land.

"No!" cried Annie. "Over there! The beach!" And she yanked at the fur as hard as she could.

The tigrish's muscles tightened and his fur bristled like dried grass. He slowed. Eventually, Annie felt him turn.

There was the red-and-green seaweed flouncing along the edge of the wet sand like a frill, and a feast of white shells broken open by seagulls. Then—yes, she knew it!—there they were: Mr. and Mrs. Hedge. They seemed so much smaller out here, away from the hedge at the edge of her garden, so much *less*.

Robbie waved, and Annie called out their names, and the tigrish circled once and dropped on to the beach. No, that wasn't right. The tigrish eased into the sand, looking lighter and sandier as he did, the wings rasping as they folded somehow into the giant body.

Mrs. Hedge stepped from behind Mr. Hedge. She moved like a goose or a duck, as if she were still uncertain about walking. "Annie? Robbie?"

Annie was already on the sand and running towards her friends. "I found you. I knew I would," she cried, crashing into them, her mouth full of leaves.

"Oh Annie, love." Mrs. Hedge's voice was higher and clearer than it was when she was surrounded by other plants. "The tigrish—"

"It's all right, really it is. I think the tigrish wants to help."

Mrs. Hedge was frowning. "You were flying," she said. "I didn't know Annies could fly."

"I didn't know hedges could walk," said Annie.

"We looked everywhere for Bud and the other babies," said Mr. Hedge, "but the nest has disappeared. I think it's lost."

"No!" said Robbie. "I can find it."

"Well, if anyone can, Robbie, it's you." Mrs. Hedge peered closer. "Goodness, you're turning into a shrub. How extraordinary."

"Oh no, it's weed from the stream," said Robbie, lifting his tee-shirt and wiping his face. "I…I fell in."

A giggle pushed its way out of Annie's throat, and Robbie made a little snort in reply. They tried not to look at each other.

"The problem is," said Mr. Hedge, "we can't move very fast, and everything here is so...*unexpected*, it's hard to know what to do, where to look. We can't do this on our own."

Annie found herself looking down at her hands, especially the one with the sunshine in it. It felt warmer than her other hand.

"Have you ever flown, Mr. Hedge?" she said.

*

The tigrish crouched low while the Hedges climbed on, and didn't once growl or groan. The Hedges, on the other hand, sounded like a bonfire, their branches crackling against each other and their leaves rustling furiously. Mrs. Hedge squeaked each time she slipped, and Mr. Hedge let out the odd "Humphrey!" Annie was worried they'd scratch the tigrish and he might roar at them or tip them off and fly away, but the tigrish didn't make a sound or move a muscle. Or maybe there was a slight growl, a very small slightly cross one? It came and went so quickly, Annie wasn't sure.

At last, they were ready. Robbie at the front holding on to the tigrish's shoulders, Annie behind him and,

CHAPTER 13

To the lighthouse

Up high, outside the light room at the top of the lighthouse, nestling at the edge of the balcony, just under the handrail, was what looked like a small mossy cup.

Something moved.

"Oh my," cried Mrs. Hedge, prodding Annie. "It's Bud."

"Bud!" shrieked Robbie.

"Well, I'll be...!" roared Mr. Hedge from the back. "What the blazes is that nest doing there?"

The tigrish made one last deep swoop and landed right

in front of the lighthouse door. As before, he seemed to sink into the stones rather than land on them, his great body tensing only slightly before relaxing into a crouch so Annie and Robbie and the Hedges could clamber off.

Annie sniffed. Was that maple syrup? She leaned towards the tigrish. Definitely maple syrup. And butter and lemon juice and the eggy smell of cooked pancakes. Her father liked to make them for breakfast. Annie's stomach rumbled. Robbie looked at her—he'd heard it. Annie swallowed and tried to concentrate on the baby birds.

"They'll be hungrier than us, Robbie. They haven't had you finding things for them to eat."

"Hmmm," said Robbie. He didn't sound sure.

"How do we get up there?" said Mrs. Hedge, blinking up at the lighthouse. She looked so small all of a sudden, and it wasn't just that she was standing beside a tall lighthouse. There was something about her that was less *solid*.

Annie didn't have time to think about it. She had a feeling they needed to hurry. She turned and ran for the lighthouse door, grabbed the handle, twisted and pulled. It didn't move. Was it locked? She grabbed with both hands and twisted harder. At last she felt the door give inside its frame and open.

Annie looked to see if the others were following. Robbie had stopped to look at the ground, but the tigrish was there, and behind the tigrish was Mrs. Hedge, her branches tucked in around the middle as if to hold herself in. In the air, a scatter of leaves. Annie thought how pretty it was, and wondered if that's what happened to a tree when it walked, in the same way a person dropped strands of hair and buttons and bits of thread. Behind Mrs. Hedge was Mr. Hedge. His leaves were curled tight like shiny green tongues, and he was puffing even though he wasn't walking fast.

"Mr. and Mrs. Hedge, are you all right?"

"Box of birds," said Mrs. Hedge, and then she started giggling, which made more leaves come away from her branches and float to the ground. She stopped walking and stood on the spot for a moment, leaning slightly to one side like a much older tree.

Annie could hear a light scraping sound above her. She looked up but couldn't see the nest.

Mrs. Hedge followed her eyes. "Do you think they're all right, Annie?" Her voice sounded gaspy.

For the first time, Annie felt stronger than the Hedges. She knew she had to—what did Mr. Hedge say?—shelter and protect them. Like she did with Robbie. Protecting someone was a different job from making sure they were okay, thought Annie. It meant you had to be bigger than yourself, not physically bigger exactly, but big *inside your head*.

She looked at her hands to see if they agreed. For the first time ever, they looked the sort of hands that could do the sorts of things her parents did. She thought of the way her mother knitted—so quickly and not even looking—or the way she peeled an apple with not a shred of peel left on the white, then cut it into paper-thin slices. She thought of her father's hands lighting the lighthouse lamp, cupping the flame so it grew.

"I am one of the last lighthouse keepers," he'd tell the family, "and I do it the old way, by hand. Some people think machines can do the jobs of people, but while machines can turn things on and off at the right time, they don't know how to tend a light properly. A light's like a plant—it needs what a plant needs."

"Water?" Annie asked once.

"Sunlight," he said. "After I extinguish the lamp in the morning, I step on to the balcony and open my hand to take a handful of sunlight to keep for later. At dusk, when I light the lamp again, I drop the sun into it."

And that's when Annie understood what was happening.

"Mrs. Hedge! You're drying out!"

Mrs. Hedge looked down. Lifted one branch and then another.

"No roots, no water," said Mr. Hedge, the "rs" rolling for longer than usual as he realized what had happened. "I didn't think—"

"There's a rainwater tank out the back," said Annie, "and I think there's a bucket."

"I'm not standing in a bucket," said Mrs. Hedge.

"Yes, you are," said Mr. Hedge, "and I will, too."

"We need to get to the fantails." Mrs. Hedge was trembling now.

Mr. Hedge stepped forward, reached for one of her branches, and held it. "Annie and Robbie can go. They've got proper legs, and legs are what's needed to get up inside that lighthouse and help the little birds. But first, the water."

As they ran—loppity, lop-loppity—around the lighthouse, Annie looked up to see if her father was watching. There was no one on the balcony, no one polishing the windows. No one working on the lamp from what she could see. She felt one of her boots catch on a rock. She looked down. How long her shadow was, and Robbie's. It was getting late.

A seagull dropped a mussel in front of Robbie and

shrieked at him when he stepped over it. Another seagull landed and tried to grab the mussel, so there were two birds shrieking now, arguing like cicadas. No cicadas, though, because there were no trees. Annie almost missed them.

"Here," said Robbie. "I found it." He was pushing a bucket into her hands.

They filled it up until it was too heavy to fill further; then, taking a side each, they walked it back to the Hedges. The metal bucket knocked against their calves and sloshed water on their legs. Robbie didn't complain once.

"Sore arm," he said, putting the bucket down at last and sitting beside it. "Hungry," he said then, holding his stomach, and finally, in a very small voice, "Mama."

Annie was squeezing her hands to get the blood back into them. "Yes, soon. Promise. We'll go home. After we bring back the birds."

"You first," said Mr. Hedge to Mrs. Hedge, and he pointed at the bucket.

"But—" said Mrs. Hedge.

"I can wait." And a small brave smile pushed itself between Mr. Hedge's branches. "Annie, you go and find Bud. Robbie, stay right here, mate. You need to rest."

CHAPTER 14

Hickory dickory

The smell in the room at the bottom of the lighthouse was of cold and cast iron and kerosene. The walls with their iron ribs seemed taller than usual, and the lighthouse stairs, winding up the far wall, were steeper than Annie remembered. Two kerosene drums—half her height—waited to be carried up to fuel the lamp. The sweet gassy smell of kerosene was insistent. Did it usually smell like this? It was as if Annie were noticing the lighthouse for the first time. Maybe with her dad there she didn't need to notice.

Above her head was a trapdoor with a loop of cable hanging through it. She knew it went all the way up through the middle of the lighthouse and that, attached to it, right at the top, was an iron weight. Her father hauled the cable up during the night, and let it fall back through the trapdoors, floor by floor, turning the giant cogs which turned the lamp. In the morning, he'd bring it up again ready for the night.

Not for the first time Annie thought that the lighthouse was like a giant grandfather clock with a pendulum and a mouse running up the middle. *Hickory dickory dock.* And she was the mouse. But this time she felt like a very tiny, unimportant mouse.

But, thought Annie, if the weight was at the top of the lighthouse now, it must have been pulled up in the morning. Which meant nothing bad had happened to their dad in the night. Maybe he'd just got busy and lost track of the time. Maybe he'd forgotten to draw the curtains…

No, that was all wrong. Her father never forgot anything at the lighthouse. He said it was always kept *ship shape*, which meant nothing was out of place, nothing was forgotten.

"Dad!" she called, but her voice sounded like one of the heavy bolts holding the lighthouse wall together.

It hit the sides of the room and fell at her feet. She tried again. This time there was an echo: *Dad.*

"I'm here," she called.

Here.

It bounced up the iron stairs all the way to the top. *Here. Here. Here.*

She waited.

Nothing.

Tried again, but louder.

"Dad!"

Dad. Dad. Dad.

"Are you there?"

There. There. There.

Annie felt her toes twitch in her boots. She had to start climbing. There were eighty steps to the top—twenty to the first floor, then fourteen to each floor after that, and four to the light room. She'd counted them so many times. With her father, it was fun climbing and counting; without him, there was too much cold and iron, and the stairs seemed too steep and too many.

Eighty.

Annie felt rather than saw the tigrish following her. She heard him groan as he tried to squeeze in.

"It's too small for you in here," she said. "You'll

get stuck. Mr. and Mrs. Hedge and Robbie need your help. Stay."

The tigrish gave her a long low look like the one Annie had just given Mr. Hedge, and then pulled back so he was on the other side of the door. She could see him waiting there, a huge paw resting on the step, the claws tucked neatly in. Annie cleared her throat.

"I won't be long," she said. "I know where to go. I'll be fine." And saying it out loud like that made her think it might be true.

She put her right foot firmly on the bottom stair, and the metal rang out like a bell. She grabbed the handrail on either side and pulled herself up four steps before stopping and looking back. She wished the tigrish had stayed now, just in case. She couldn't think what the "just in case" might be, except that it *might* have something to do with the echo, or it might be the small scraping sound she thought she could hear somewhere up above. Annie strained her ears, but there were only splashing sounds now, and they came from outside.

Thinking of Mrs. Hedge standing in the bucket with her leaves plumping up made Annie feel better. She kept climbing.

Counting out loud made it easier. At twenty, she reached the first floor: wooden planks to walk on, some

would flare and fill the glass dome, and spill through the lenses in a single powerful beam.

Annie stopped at the next window and looked out. Mr. Hedge was in the bucket. His leaves had uncurled—they looked like mirrors again—and Mrs. Hedge seemed to be dancing nearby. Robbie was sitting beside the bucket, watching Mrs. Hedge. The tigrish was pacing and watching the lighthouse. Annie tapped the window. Was anyone watching Robbie? What if he wandered off? There were so many rocks and places to fall. She could hear the waves guzzling out there, eating the rocks and anyone who fell in.

Annie tapped the window and called their names. They couldn't hear her. She'd just have to hurry. The cold of the iron walls had gone into her spine and made little bumps on her bare arms. The smell of kerosene was so strong it made her feel a bit sick. It was never like this, ever. She remembered her father swishing some over the bonfire at home, then making her stand back while he threw on a match. "You must never touch this stuff," he'd said. "Even the *smell* of it is dangerous. Make a mistake and you can go up in smoke." *Click* went his fingers. "Like that."

Something had happened to him, she was sure of it now.

"Dad!" Annie tried again, but her voice jousted with the iron stairs and the iron walls and crashed to the ground. Nothing. All Annie could hear were the sort of sounds she heard sitting on the swing at home. The rush of air, metal creaks. And now a bunch of seagulls making that noise people make when they're pretending to laugh. Another breath in... *Stop it, Annie, crying didn't help anyone.*

The final two curves of the spiral staircase were the steepest of all. Her arms ached from pulling her body up. Step. By. Step. She pushed on, feeling the stairs with her feet because it was too dark to see now. And here she was at last at the top, the place where the hatchlings waited for her, where her father might be.

CHAPTER 15

The lamp

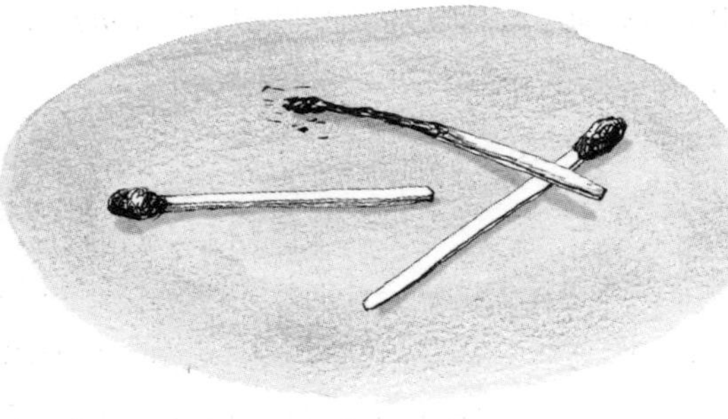

The light room was only four more steps away.

Annie heard a sound on the stairs as if someone were following her. Or was it an echo of her own feet? Out of the corner of her eye, something flickered. A moth? A mouse? Something bigger? Annie pushed her back against the wall of the lighthouse and stared hard into the dark spiral she'd climbed for the first time on her own.

Was she imagining things? Her hands—one of them still warm with the sunshine she was holding—

were pressed against the iron wall. She could feel the metal ribs and the metal nuts and bolts that held them together. That's when daylight took off from the window like a bird, and flew away leaving Annie in darkness. It wasn't, though, not really. Not *dark* dark, like the woods. She thought of her mother holding her hand and pointing at the stars, and Annie knew she just had to wait with her back against the wall until her eyes could pick things out.

There they were! A kerosene tank with a tap. A bookshelf. Three books. A chair with a seat so saggy it almost touched the ground. The chair where her father sat in the long nights. Annie nudged herself onwards.

One—the steps here were narrower.

Two—the steps here were steeper.

Three—her legs here were tireder.

Four—the light room, at last.

The door was open, and the smell of kerosene jumped up and grabbed her by the chest. Annie put her hand over her nose and mouth and blinked to stop her eyes watering.

The lamp stood up on its platform inside the lenses of polished glass. She could see the outlines of the cogs underneath that turned it, a coil of rope, her father's white coffee mug…

...something shiny...

—water?—

...something else beside it...

Annie's scream jangled around the glassy room. She took a sobbing breath to scream again, and it felt as if the whole of the lighthouse were sucking in air with her. And with it came a rush of something licorishy and *solid*. Up the stairs and pushing past, pulling her with it, a shadow that would swamp a mouse.

Tigrish.

*

A different kind of light had arrived with the tigrish, and it lit up the puddle of kerosene—for that's what it was—and the fallen kerosene drum that had spilled, and Annie's father curled on his side, his arm under his head, his hair sticking up. He looked like he was asleep.

The tigrish was nuzzling him, but he wasn't waking.

"Dad?" Annie dropped to her knees and began nuzzling, too. "Can you hear me?" Close to the ground, the kerosene made her eyes water badly. She could smell the tigrish breath, too, like burnt toast with peanut butter on it. How had he got in here?

The tigrish lifted a paw and patted at her father like a cat with a mouse.

"What are you doing?" said Annie, rubbing and

rubbing her eyes. She sounded cross. She felt sick, really. Sick and scared.

The tigrish patted her father again and watched as he slumped on to his back, his head lolling, his eyes still shut. There was an egg-sized lump on his forehead.

"Don't hurt him!" Annie said, and burst into tears. Then she felt silly straight away. The tigrish was not going to hurt her father. She could see that from the softness about his face and ears, and something that was like sadness there. But she was sad, too. Sadder. And she had no idea what to do.

"I think we need to move him. It's horrible here, he can't breathe."

She stood, shakily, then leaned down and picked up one of her father's arms. The tigrish took the other arm in the soft outer part of his mouth. Annie looked at the tigrish and the tigrish looked at Annie, and then they pulled.

He was too heavy at first. Annie put her dad's arm down and picked it up again. This time she felt the tigrish take most of the weight. Three good pulls, and they'd hauled her father to the door and settled him on his side. That's when Annie saw the old cleaning towels and rubber gloves, and had another idea. The tigrish was pacing back and forward, making low growling noises and looking up at the lamp. He wanted her to hurry, but Annie wouldn't hurry. She took the towels to the puddle, put on the gloves, and wiped and wiped until the puddle had gone. She remembered what her father had said at the bonfire. The click of his fingers as he said it.

Anyway, it was done now and the towels smelled disgusting. Annie looked for somewhere to put them. The only place she could think of was the trapdoor for the cable. It was dark, very dark, down there. She heard the towels snag on the cable and fall with a flump on the wooden floor below.

Annie tried to go to her father again, but the tigrish stood in the way. He looked at the steps leading up to the glass dome.

"What?" she said.

The tigrish didn't move.

"The lamp?" said Annie at last.

The tigrish gave a long low growl and looked her in the eye.

"You want *me* to do it? I don't know what to do. Not really. There are all these things…to light it…and you need…"

Sunlight.

Annie thought suddenly of the gap in the hedge.

Her hands and the light she'd kept.

"I have it. It's here." And Annie thrust her right hand under the tigrish's leathery muzzle.

What was that? A drop of liquid shimmered like wet gold across her palm. She closed it again quickly. Gold?

Annie didn't have time to think.

The tigrish seemed to nudge her across the floor to the lamp and up the steps to the door of the glass dome. Annie stepped in. No dancing light, no rainbows today. The matches in their small hard box.

"Okay," she said. "I'll try."

She felt for the knob under the lamp and turned it until she could hear the kerosene hiss. Then she struck a match, once, *hard* against the side of the box. The red tip splintered and broke. Annie tried another one.

It sprung up briefly—a tiny flame—sputtered and… died.

The third time, the flame grew and bobbed hopefully like Bud in his nest. Annie held it to the wick under the lamp. It sputtered, flared and…seemed to settle.

"It worked!" said Annie.

Behind her, the tigrish pushed a *shuf* of air through his nostrils. She looked around and he was glowing, right to the tips of his fur—the blue-gold light like the hottest part of a fire.

"Now we have to wait," she said. "Everything has to be just right before we add the sunlight."

Her father said he sang a little song in his head to remember how long the waiting had to be. Annie already had a song in her head that would do: *Hickory dickory dock—the mouse ran up the clock—the clock struck one, the mouse ran down—hickory dickory dock.* She leaned forward, holding her right hand above the small flame. She turned it over.

The drop of saved sunlight left her hand, and there was a whoosh as the wick grew white, and then whiter still. Annie's eyes flared white too until she could see nothing *but* white. She shut them and felt her way out of the glass dome. Standing on the floor of the light room, she blinked and blinked until she could see again.

Light was filling the dome above her like milk in a glass, and then being sucked out like a single giant straw into the mouth of the night sky. Out there, thought Annie, a ship will see it and know to steer away from the rocks and the people on board will sleep safely in their beds. She went to the trapdoor and released the cable so the weight would start to fall. It began making its way through, floor by floor, and the lamp started to turn.

Annie felt dizzy looking down. She teetered and

put out a hand to stop herself from falling. It was the hand—the one with the sunshine in it. Was there still something there? She felt a tug like a fish on a hook.

Annie went to her father and knelt beside him. Her hand pulsed. Her throat felt rigid. Her ears whooshed with the sound of the lamp burning and her own heart beating. Or was it her father's? She couldn't separate them. The lamp. Her heart. Her father's heart. There was nothing else for it.

Arm out stiffly in front of her, hand cupped over the dear bruised face, eyes shut…she needed something magic to say. *Hickory dickory dock*…no, that wouldn't do at all. Annie could feel a rush of warm breath on the back of her legs—of course, the most magical word she knew.

Tigrish, she said, and turned her hand over.

The tiniest filament of sunlight hung in the air briefly, goldenly—and fell.

CHAPTER 16

Finding Bud

Mr. Hedge had clambered from the bucket of water and Mrs. Hedge was about to climb in. They weren't sure what else to do. They didn't have the fantails and they didn't have Annie, and Robbie had gone to sleep at last in a little huddle on the ground. And now the tigrish had galloped away up the stairs.

"Can you see them, Mr. Hedge?" said Mrs. Hedge, and she didn't know whether she meant the fantails or Annie and the tigrish. Any of them would do. She was feeling weepy. All that water she'd drunk hadn't helped.

"I can just see the nest, love, or at least some of it poking from the balcony. It's too dark to see much more. I think the babies are safe, but Annie hasn't got to them yet."

"I'm so worried," said Mrs. Hedge. "When she screamed I—"

"The tigrish went to her," said Mr. Hedge. "The tigrish will help."

"But what if he can't? What's happening?"

It was the lighthouse that answered her. A beam of white light spilled from its windows as bright as anything Mrs. Hedge had ever seen. It turned, and as it turned it shone over the rocks and the sea and out as far as a light could go.

The two Hedges stood branch-in-branch, watching. The light made no sound but it *felt* like somebody laughing, or like lemonade being poured into a cup.

It blinked four times.

*

Annie's father spluttered and opened his eyes.

"You're alive!" shouted Annie.

He wasn't looking at her. He was looking at the tigrish, and now he was holding up his hand to show Annie to wait. She looked from one to the other for as long as it took her to understand. *They knew each other.*

She saw her father nod and the tigrish nod back, and then, like butter, he melted from the room. One minute the tigrish was there, and then he wasn't, and instead of a golden body filling the narrow space and giving off its own golden light, there was just thin air and the single beam of white light that hurtled from the light room and out across the sea.

"He won't go far," said her father.

"Dad!" And Annie tried to hug him.

"Ouch."

"Sorry—"

"No, it's not you, it's my head."

"Are you all right?" said Annie. The light from the lamp stroked his face in passing—the egg-shaped bruise, the light fuzz on his chin—gently, as if it cared.

Annie was thinking about this when her father sat up like Robbie did, quick as a spring, and said, "The lamp! *Who on earth—?*"

"Me," said Annie. "I did it."

He was struggling to stand.

"It's all done. I cleaned up the kerosene, too."

"Kerosene?" Her father was sniffing the air, and then he was on his feet and tripping over the fallen drum. He hauled it upright and had to lean against the wall to get his breath back.

"I remember now," he said. "I heard an earthquake coming over the fields and the rocks, and then everything was shaking. It was like the lighthouse was made of rubber. The drum must have fallen over then. It was full and I'd just opened it, and when I turned around...I suppose I slipped—" Her father put his hand up to his head and felt the lump there. "Stupid, stupid," he said. Then one at a time, two feet on each step, he walked up to the glass dome.

Annie saw him look in at the lamp, adjust something, nod, then walk down the steps backwards. He opened his arms wide for her.

"Good job," he said. "You can work for me any time," and hugged Annie tight. Then he took a small tin from his pocket and opened it. Licorice. She put one in her mouth.

"How did you know to come?" he said.

"I didn't. The tigrish came to get me to look for the baby fantails. There was a terrible wind which took the hatchlings away, and Mr. and Mrs. Hedge were really upset—so upset they uprooted themselves and walked all the way to the sea, looking for the babies..."

Annie looked closely at her father, but he didn't seem surprised by anything she was saying. "I know you tell me not to go through the hedge, but I was

closer, she could see the way his wings were spread over the sides of the nest, his beak open and breathing fast.

"I've come to get the babies," Annie said, and the bird stopped puffing for a moment. She heard a tiny sound like a rustle or a squeak.

"Pick."

The father fantail tucked in one wing and then the other. He blinked.

"Pick."

Annie reached out and held on to the nest with both hands.

"Me."

"Bud!" she said, and gave a small tug. She couldn't see Bud but she could hear him. The nest wouldn't come. She tugged again. She heard her father say something but it didn't make any sense, not with the little bird voices so close. There was a moment when she was looking into the eyes of the father bird, and then she wasn't looking any more, and the nest and the fantails were falling out of her hands.

Annie couldn't scream. She just stood with her mouth open, making no sound at all. It was like *it was her* falling through the air.

She pushed past her father. Ran for the stairs. Clutched the handrail tightly, each step like thunder.

CHAPTER 17

What Hedges do

At the bottom of the stairs, the door was wide open. Annie fell through it and into Mr. and Mrs. Hedge.

"The babies!" said Annie. "I dropped them! They slipped out of my fingers—did you see—?" She looked hopelessly at the ground and then up at the milky night sky lit by the roving light at the top of the lighthouse. No moon, no stars, no nest.

"Me," said Mrs. Hedge.

"What did you say, Mrs. Hedge?"

Mrs. Hedge opened her branches wide, and there it

was, the nest and the father fantail and the hatchlings getting louder by the second. "Pick! Pick! Pick! Me!" they shouted.

"One thing we Hedges are good at," said Mr. Hedge proudly, "is catching things. We're *r-r*-ready whatever happens."

"*R-r-r*-ready for anything!" said Annie. "You saved the baby birds."

"Haven't lost one yet," said Mr. Hedge. "Never will."

"You did find them, Annie!" It was Robbie, wide awake now and jumping from foot to foot, his shinies rattling. Then he was running for his father who was stepping through the lighthouse door.

"Yes Annie, love, well done," said Mrs. Hedge.

Annie could see the mouth saying the words this time. A mouth shaped like a leaf, or a leaf shaped like a mouth. She couldn't be sure which. "But *imagine* if you hadn't been standing here, Mrs. Hedge," she said. "What would have happened then?"

Annie heard a restless moan behind her. She turned. The tigrish was close by, watching, half in and half out of the night shadow of the lighthouse. Her father said he wouldn't go far. She lifted her hand.

"Thank you," she said. The tigrish dipped his head and walked off a little distance without making a sound.

Annie's father was talking into the radio-telephone just inside the door of the lighthouse, with Robbie holding on to his leg; Annie could faintly hear her mother's voice, crackly and upset, and her father's voice, low and explainy. She thought of the terrible sounds Mrs. Hedge had made when the nest flew away, and she wondered if her mother had made the same sounds when she'd woken up and found Annie- and Robbie-shaped gaps in the garden.

Time to go home. Annie walked past the Hedges, murmuring to reassure the fantails, and climbed on the dappled back of the tigrish. He crackled lightly underneath her, a creature that was dark and light, hot and cold, glowing and warm to touch, and smelling of freshly baked bread. Annie felt furiously hungry again.

The Hedges were climbing on the tigrish's back now. Their dad carried Robbie over on his shoulders and swung him up in front of Annie.

"Hold on tight, Robbie, eh?" he said. "The tigrish won't drop you, but you'll feel safer that way."

Robbie opened his mouth but Annie prodded him in the back. There are some things you tell your parents only when the time is right.

Annie's dad leaned close to the tigrish's ear and spoke quietly so Annie couldn't hear. The creature's ears twitched. The Hedges pushed and rustled, the hatchlings cheeped and the father fantail gave one short squeak. At last, Annie's father stood back, tall and pale beside the tall pale lighthouse. Annie thought she caught sight of a funnel on the horizon. Below the bank of gray clouds, there was a thin puff of smoke.

"Are you coming soon?" she said.

"I need to work here until it's light," said her father, "but I promise that as soon as I can come home I will. *You* made that possible, Annie. You and Robbie. Now hurry, it's going to start raining any minute, and your mother's waiting. By the way, I didn't tell her about the tigrish. I said I'd take you home on the front of the bike and drop you at the garden gate. We'll tell her later, when she's ready."

As they lifted off from the hard ground and into the night, a beam of white light caught them. For a brief moment the tigrish, the Hedges, the birds, Annie, Robbie—every surface, every cranny—were brightly lit. Caught in the same beam, her father's hand was waving.

A dash of rain, then, like a pencil line, and another and another. One scribbled its way across Annie's cheek.

They were on their way, out over the dark sea in a

huge swinging arc, and through the stars to the hill, the paddock and the hedge.

Annie's mother didn't see the tigrish drop into the paddock just behind the hedge, nor did she see the Hedges climb off and clamber back to the place they'd come from, or the way the tigrish, with a noise like a striking match and the whiff of something that smelled faintly of chocolate cake and candles, was gone. She saw only Annie and Robbie beside her at last in the kitchen, hugging her tightly, leaving wet greenish patches on her clothes and cheeping like hungry birds.

CHAPTER 18

Dappled Annie

The next day was Annie's birthday. She was ten and it was sunny, and the cicadas were performing an opera in the garden.

There was a chocolate cake with candles, a new hula hoop, a book on birds, and four tickets to the circus. Lew's replacement had arrived at last and had gone straight to the lighthouse, so Annie's father was sitting at the kitchen table, drinking coffee and eating pancakes, just as he'd promised. They all agreed that this was the most exciting present of all.

Her father said they could all go to the circus next weekend. "There's an acrobat who juggles hoops and fire."

"Any animals?" said Annie.

"No, circuses don't have animals these days." He smiled, reached into his pocket and pressed something damp into her hand. It was a tiny plastic ballet dancer with a real net tutu. "I think it's from that music box I found," he said.

The dancer seemed to shiver.

"Thank you," said Annie, "she's beautiful," and slipped her into her pocket.

"Something for me?" said Robbie.

His father held out his hand in a fist. Robbie touched it and the hand opened like a flower. There in the middle was a pinecone as small as a nut. Robbie looked at Annie as if to say, "Shall I tell him?"

Annie moved her head very slightly from side to side: *No—not—now*. Everyone was safe. It was her birthday. Stories about nasty trees and pinecone bombs would only upset her mother, and there would be questions, and she wouldn't be able to go off to the hedge and play. They could tell the whole story tomorrow—couldn't they?

Robbie had lost interest. He'd started lining up the

shinies to meet the pinecone. So Annie slipped away.

When she reached the hedge, but before she'd started to climb in, there was an explosion of birds, insects and shrubs singing "Happy Birthday to You." Holly carried on the longest, and Russell giggled even though no one was tickling him.

Zip-it zip-it zip-it, said the cicadas.

A blue flower dropped in front of Annie.

"From me," said George.

"Thank you," said Annie. "Oh, it's beautiful! But it's your last one..." She tried to give it back, but George waved a branch in front of her. Small blossoms, green, like miniature cauliflowers, clung there.

"Babies!" said Annie.

"Yes," said George proudly.

"As if there aren't already enough in this hedge," said Manny.

"Me," squeaked Bud.

Annie climbed up to see him. His little head wobbled blindly on its neck, his beak open, waiting. One of his brothers jabbed him with a featherless wing and Bud jabbed him back. He didn't look quite so small now.

"Bud thinks I'm a bird, Mrs. Hedge," she said. "So do the others. When will they open their eyes and see I'm a girl?"

"Give them time," said Mrs. Hedge. "They've still got a lot of eating to do."

The father fantail flew in and stuffed an insect into one of the beaks. He watched his babies for a moment in that quizzical way he had, as if he were amazed that he had all these mouths to feed, and then he danced away through Mrs. Hedge's branches and out on to the lawn.

Mrs. Hedge giggled.

"We haven't lost one yet, Mrs. Hedge," said Annie.

"No, Annie love, we haven't. Without you and Robbie…no, I don't want to think about it. Not just the birds are safe, your father is too. Here—" she slid a tigrish feather into Annie's hair— "I keep finding them in my branches." Mrs. Hedge purred or growled, Annie wasn't sure which, and for the first time she saw all of her friend's face: the eyes, the branches that made up her cheekbones, her leafy mouth, her chin, the dappled light on her forehead.

Annie stared and stared until Mrs. Hedge blushed—her leaves going a soft orange, which might have been the sun or it might not—and tried to hide herself away again.

Annie lifted her right arm and saw on there the delicate pattern of light and shadow that happened only when she was in the hedge. *Dappled Annie*, she thought. *Different from the other girls*. And for the first time she felt proud of this, not as if she had to apologize. She thought of the other girls she knew who liked skipping, and realized that she didn't like skipping. Not at all. Not even a little bit.

"Where's Annie?" said Mr. Hedge, right beside her and suddenly very loud.

"Right here," said Mrs. Hedge. Her face had mostly disappeared, except for the eyes which glimmered.

"Humph!" said Mr. Hedge. "I couldn't see you for looking, Annie. Thought you were a hedgeling. You two better get ready, we're off for a birthday picnic."

"Pick, pick, pick…" said the little birds.

"…me," squeaked Bud.

"A picnic!" said Annie, then, "Hedgeling!" Then, "No, no, Bud, you can't go—and neither can I. We said—" Was she imagining it, or was her right hand warmer than her left? *Still?*

"We're not going far," said Mrs. Hedge, taking one careful step on to the lawn and flicking her leaves back. Annie saw the nest in there with the little birds bobbing. "I've had enough of wandering. In fact," said Mrs. Hedge, "this looks like the best place for a picnic right here."

“This is the *best place* for a birthday picnic in the whole world,” said Annie. “Can Robbie come too?”

“Yes,” said Mrs. Hedge, “I’ve got a little something for him.”

The smell this time was baked apples with raisins and brown sugar and cinnamon. And custard. Annie heard the growl first, so low it was barely a growl, and felt the warm breath like an open oven on the back of her neck.

Robbie was running towards her in his boots and waving his arms and calling, “Wait for me! Wait for me!”

And Annie did.

THE END

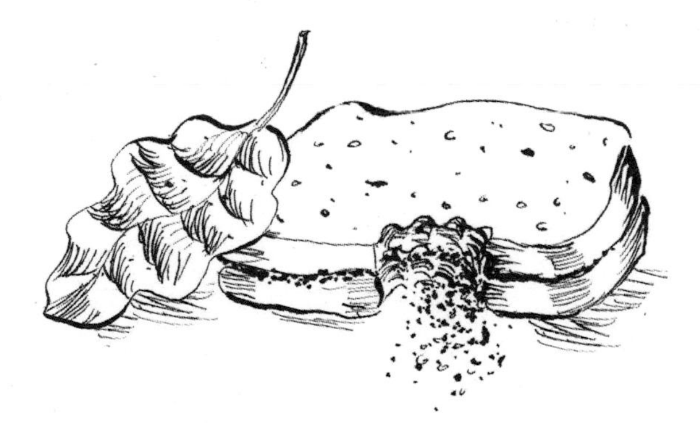

THANKS TO—

The first Annie—Annie Hayward—whose painting *Mr and Mrs Hedge went for a walk* started me off, and for sharing her talent and family with me. Ian for the olive grove: a magical place of trees, nests, and winds. Alexandra for showing me how trees talk. My brothers for our childhood, and to all the children who gave up bits of themselves for Annie and Robbie especially Issy, Paul, Adam, Libby, Daisy, Ned, Lincoln, and Carter. Lighthouse children Penny and Michelle, and their dad—last New Zealand lighthouse keeper, Grant Hinchcliff—for their stories. Jackie for opening up her archives. Castlepoint for opening its lighthouse. My first readers: Issy, Sandra P, Mum, Dad, Libby, Andy, Richard, and Stella. Julia and Jane of Gecko for their generous and imaginative publishing, Jane P for the edits, and Luke, the design. My family and friends for their love and support.